Be like Batty—read them all!

Shark and Bot

Sleepaway Champs

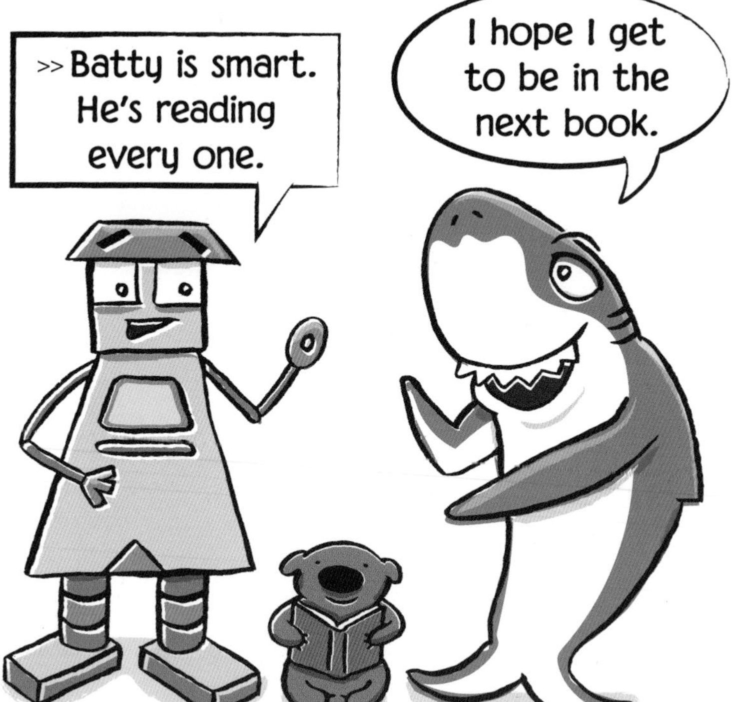
>> Batty is smart. He's reading every one.
I hope I get to be in the next book.

SHARK AND BOT 2

Sleepaway Champs

Brian Yanish

A STEPPING STONE BOOK™

Random House 🏠 New York

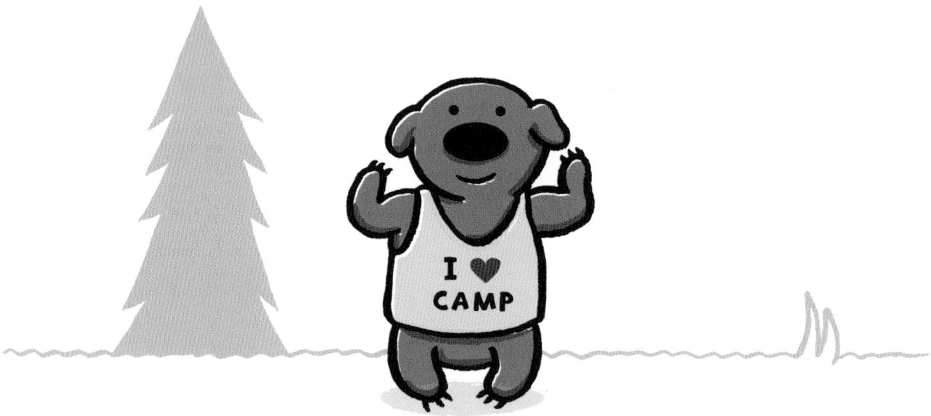
I ♥
CAMP

Photo credit pg. 80: "Vombatus Ursinus–Maria Island National Park" by JJ Harrison courtesy of Creative Commons Attribution-ShareAlike 3.0 Unported (CC BY-SA 3.0) license. No changes made. https://creativecommons.org/licenses/by-sa/3.0/deed.en.

Visit us on the Web! rhcbooks.com

Educators and librarians, for a variety of teaching tools, visit us at RHTeachersLibrarians.com

Library of Congress Cataloging-in-Publication Data is available upon request.
ISBN 978-0-593-17338-1 (hardcover) | ISBN 978-0-593-17339-8 (lib. bdg.) |
ISBN 978-0-593-17340-4 (ebook)

Book design by Jan Gerardi

MANUFACTURED IN CHINA

10 9 8 7 6 5 4 3 2 1

First Edition

For Mom and Dad

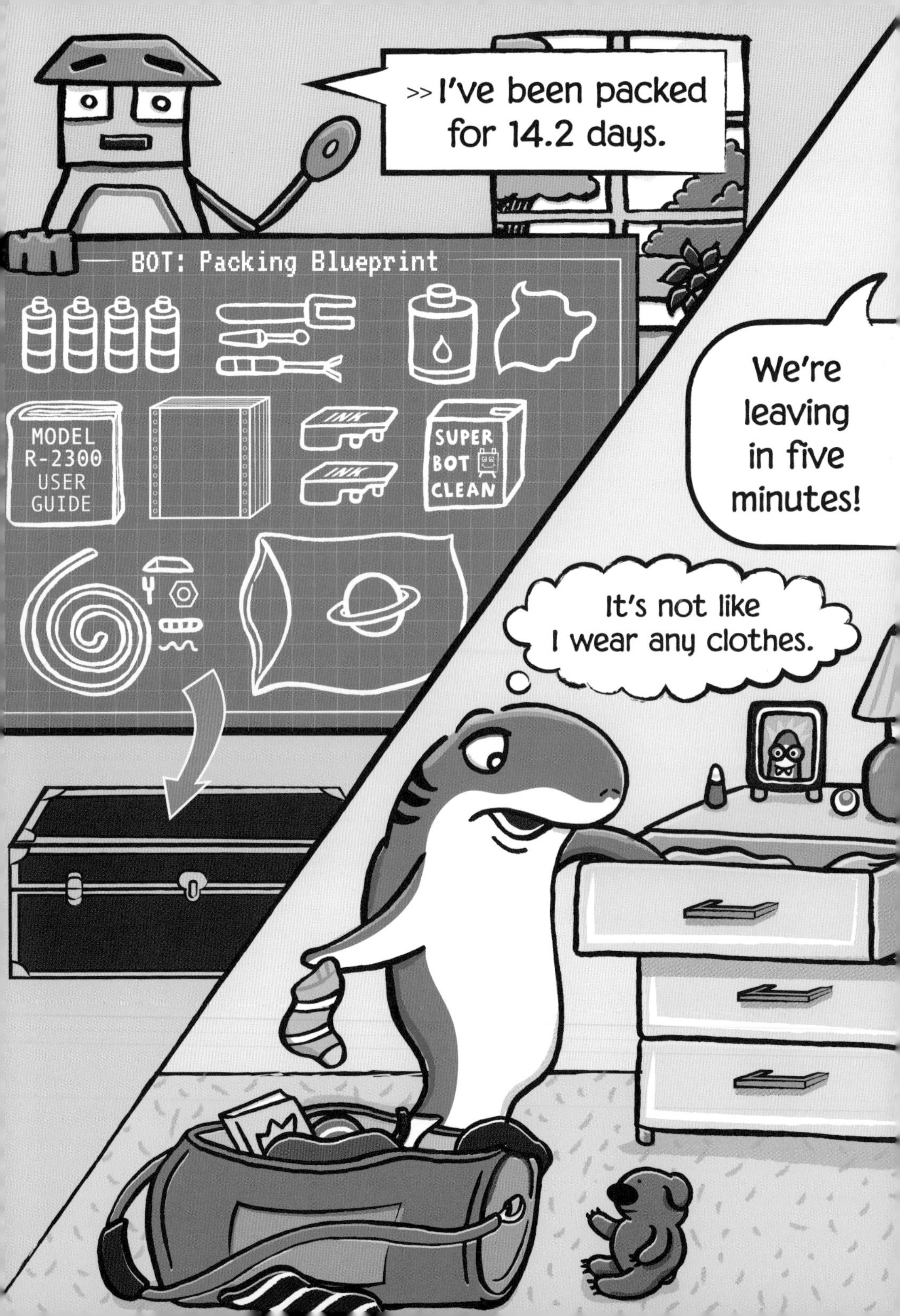

>> I've been packed for 14.2 days.
BOT: Packing Blueprint
MODEL R-2300 USER GUIDE
INK
INK
SUPER BOT CLEAN
We're leaving in five minutes!
It's not like I wear any clothes.

Contents

1. Bunkmates   1

2. Sunshine and Sparkles   7

3. Nightmares   15

4. Getting Crafty   28

5. What Did You Get?   35

6. Talent Takes Practice   43

7. Ghost Hunting   50

8. Summer Camp-ions   64

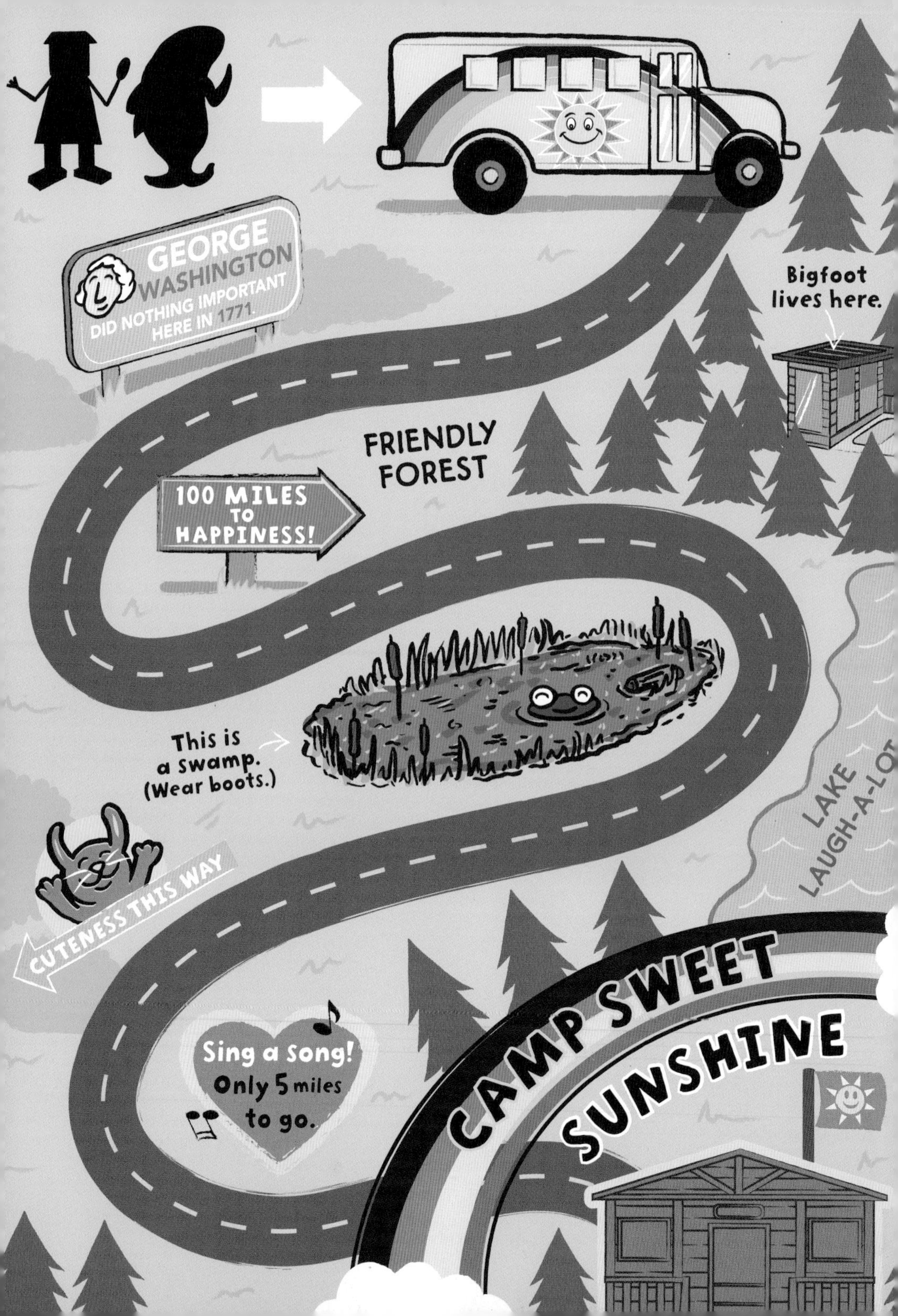

GEORGE WASHINGTON DID NOTHING IMPORTANT HERE IN 1771.
Bigfoot lives here.
FRIENDLY FOREST
100 MILES TO HAPPINESS!
This is a swamp. (Wear boots.)
LAKE LAUGH-A-LOT
CUTENESS THIS WAY
Sing a Song! Only 5 miles to go.
CAMP SWEET SUNSHINE

Chapter 1
Bunkmates

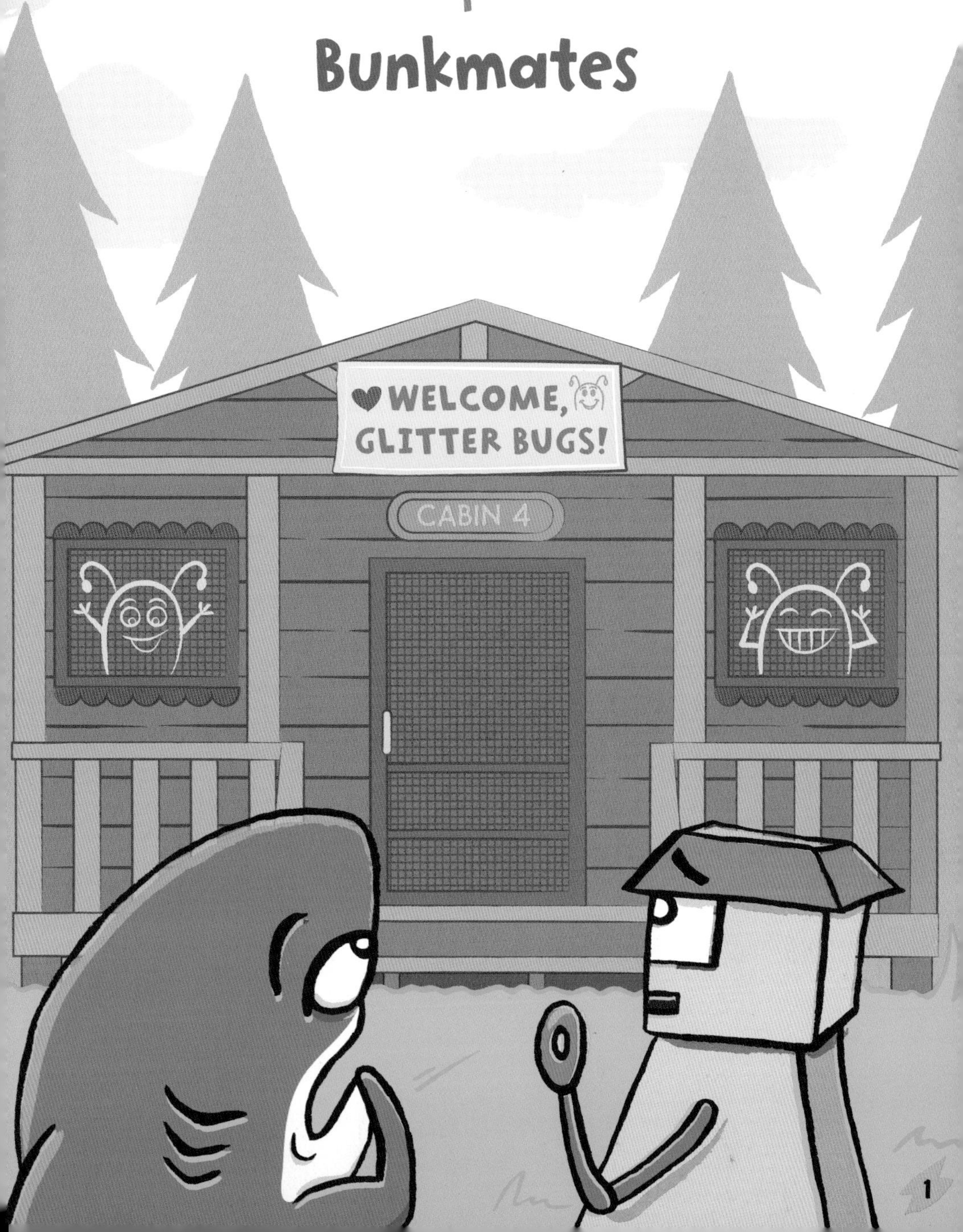
WELCOME, GLITTER BUGS!
CABIN 4

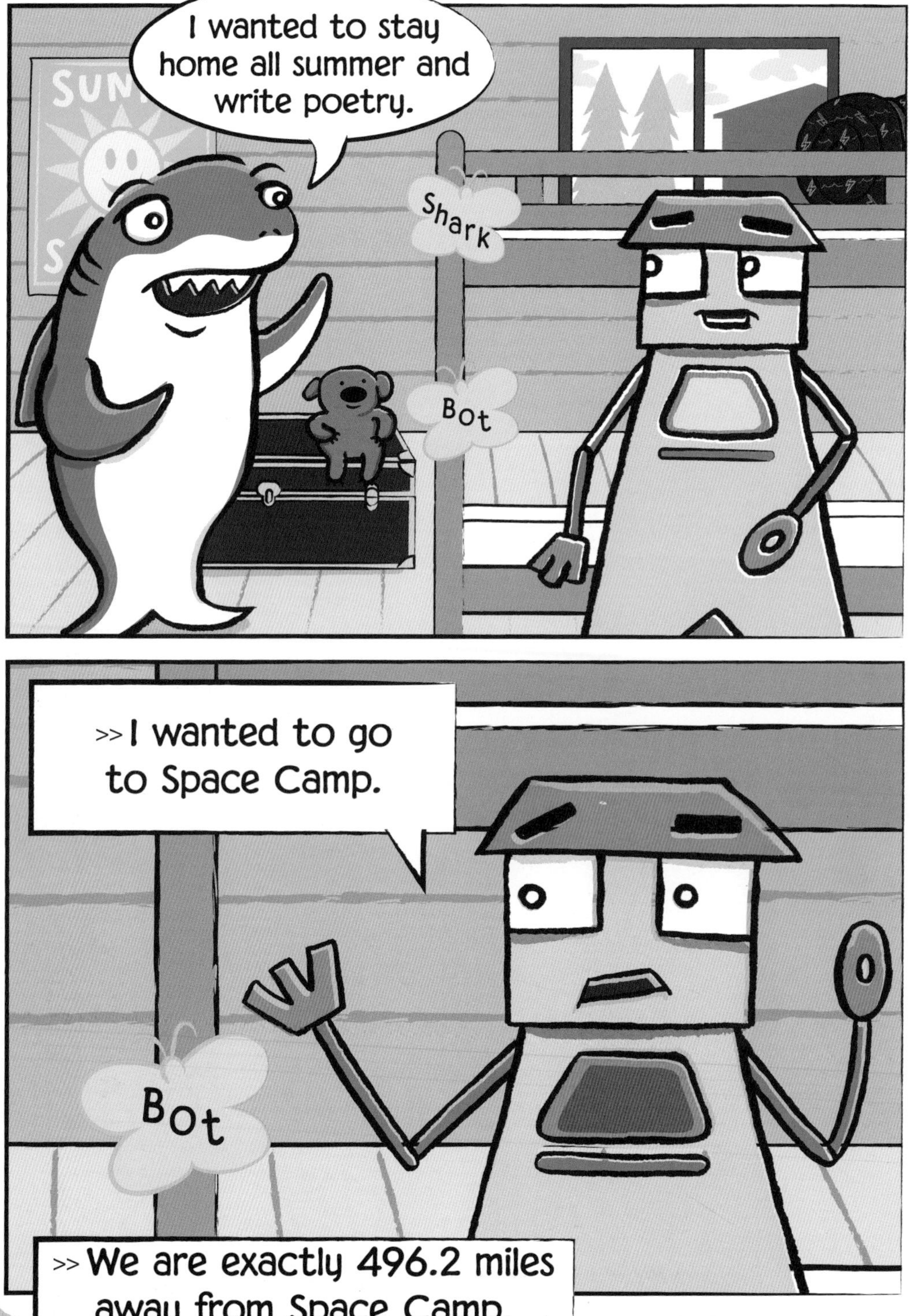
I wanted to stay home all summer and write poetry.
Shark
Bot
>>I wanted to go to Space Camp.
Bot
>>We are exactly 496.2 miles away from Space Camp.

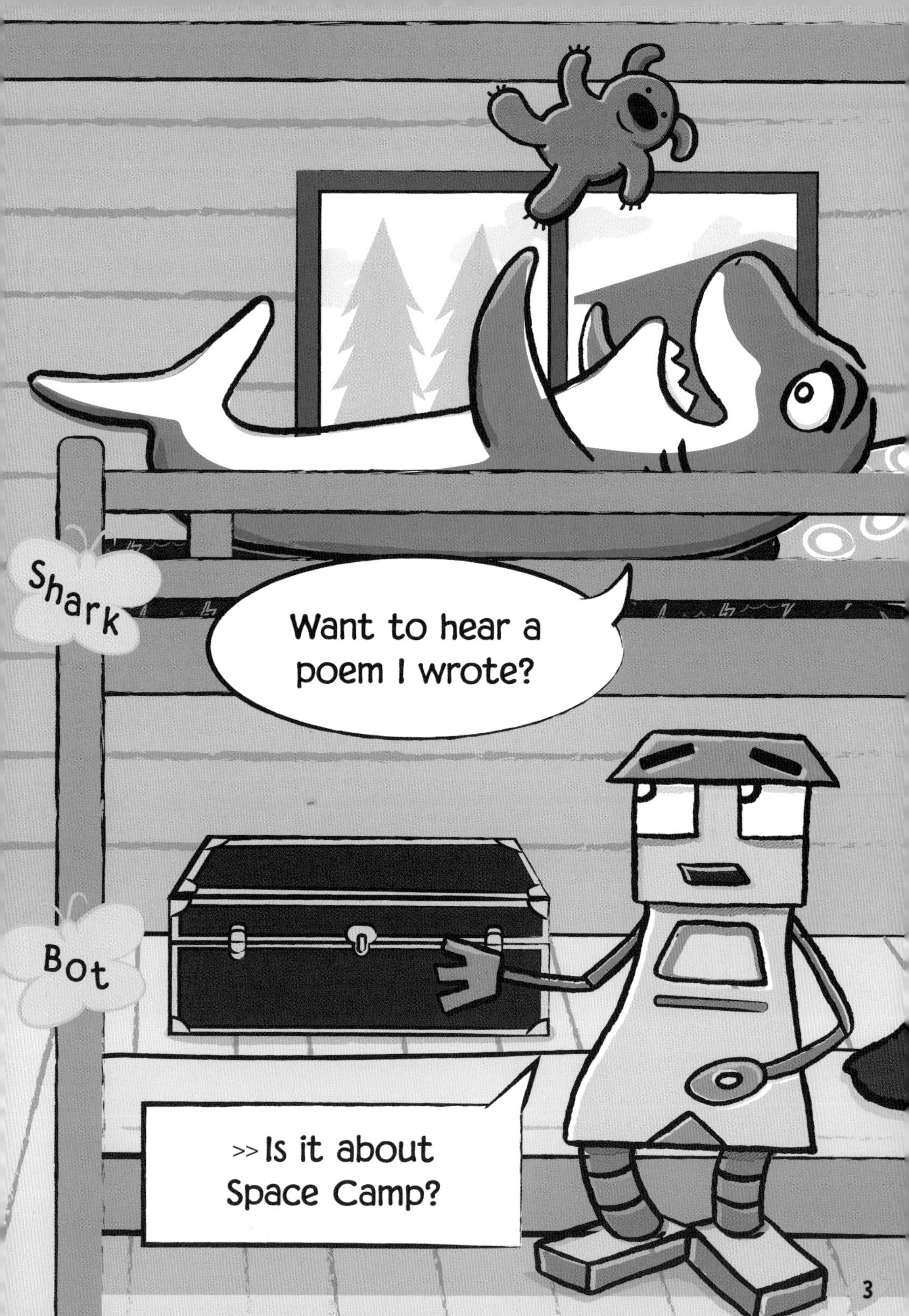
Shark
Want to hear a poem I wrote?
Bot
>> Is it about Space Camp?

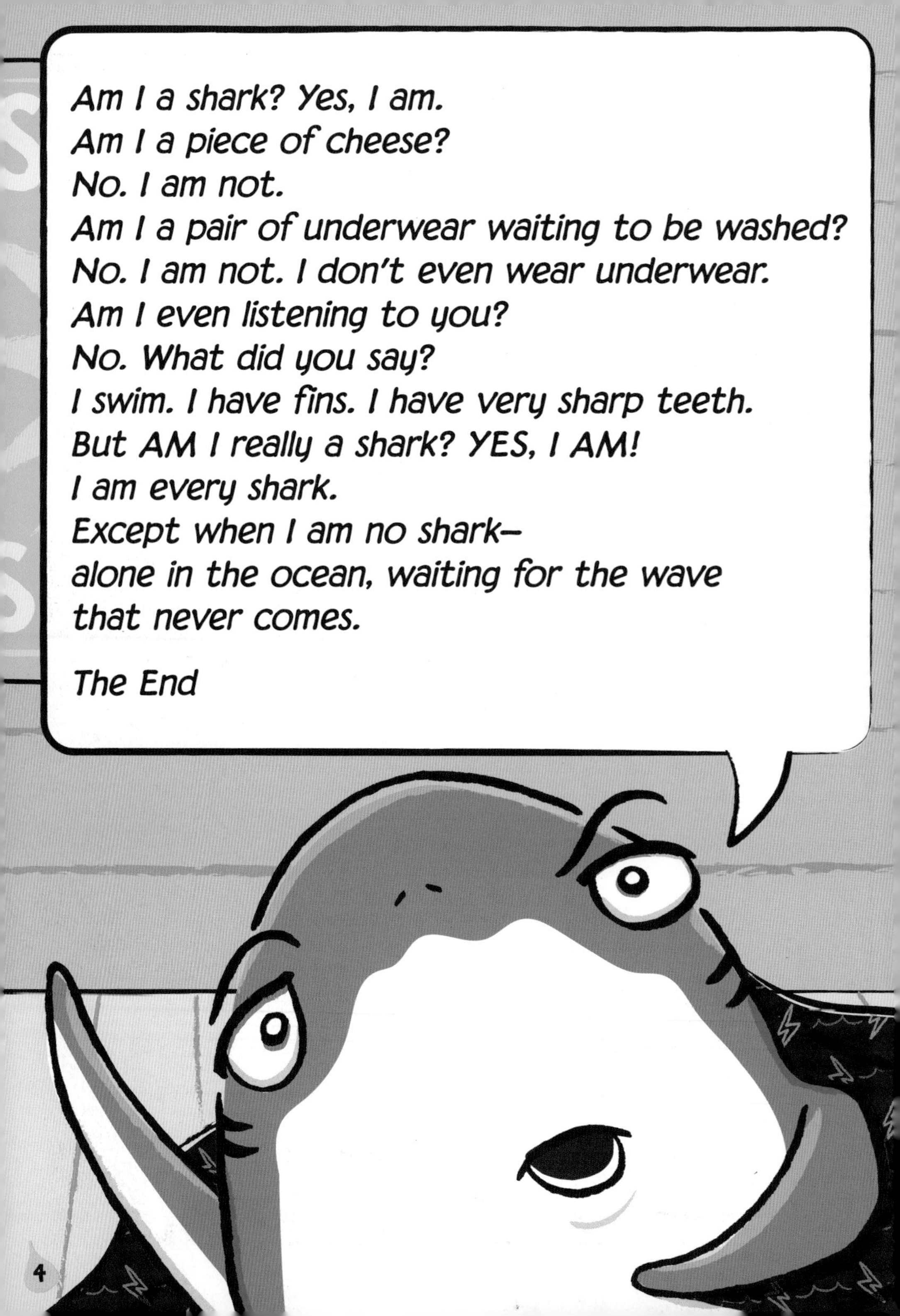
Am I a shark? Yes, I am.
Am I a piece of cheese?
No. I am not.
Am I a pair of underwear waiting to be washed?
No. I am not. I don't even wear underwear.
Am I even listening to you?
No. What did you say?
I swim. I have fins. I have very sharp teeth.
But AM I really a shark? YES, I AM!
I am every shark.
Except when I am no shark—
alone in the ocean, waiting for the wave
that never comes.
The End

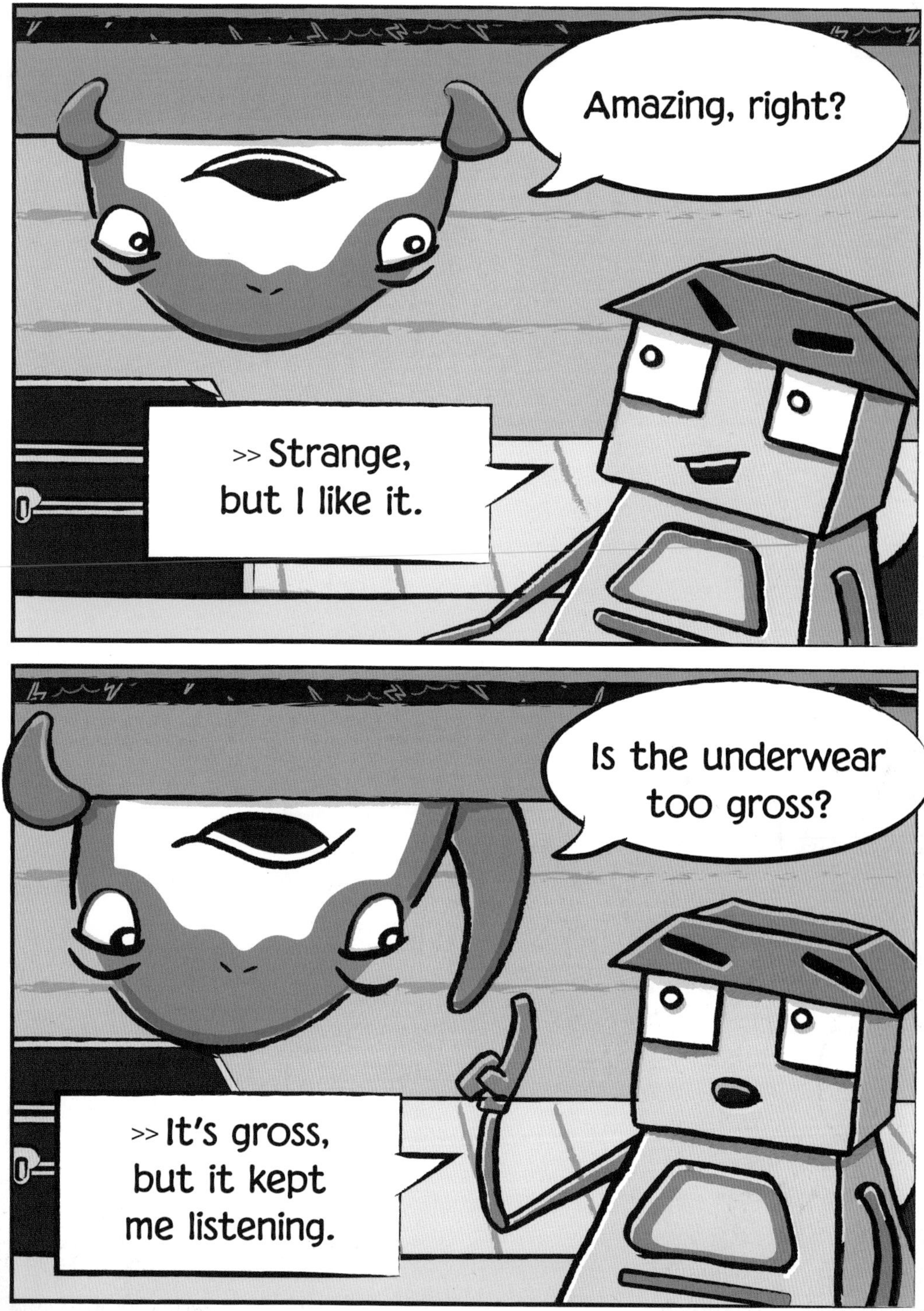
Amazing, right?
>> Strange, but I like it.
Is the underwear too gross?
>> It's gross, but it kept me listening.

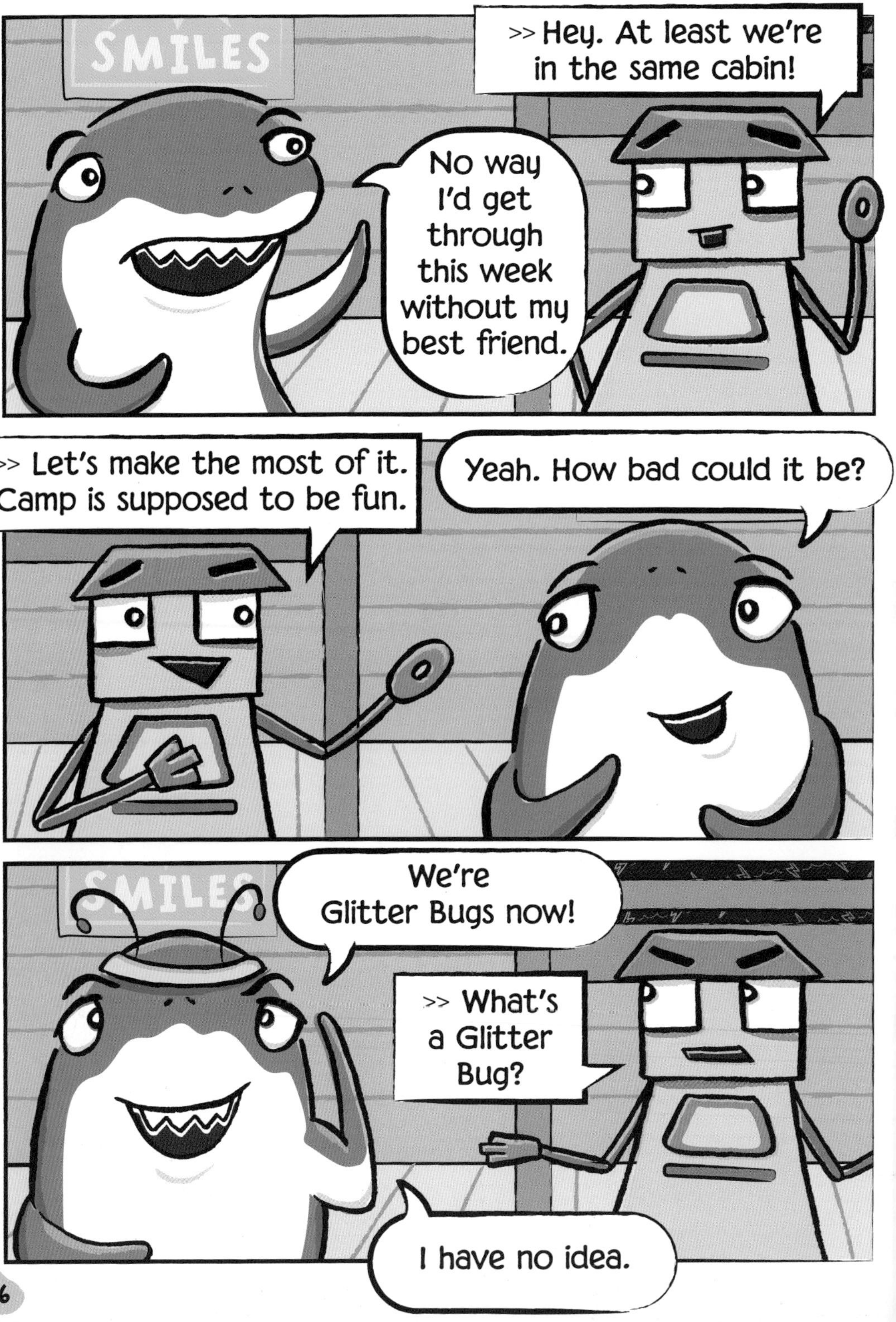

>> Hey. At least we're in the same cabin!
No way I'd get through this week without my best friend.
SMILES
>> Let's make the most of it. Camp is supposed to be fun.
Yeah. How bad could it be?
We're Glitter Bugs now!
>> What's a Glitter Bug?
I have no idea.

Chapter 2
Sunshine and Sparkles

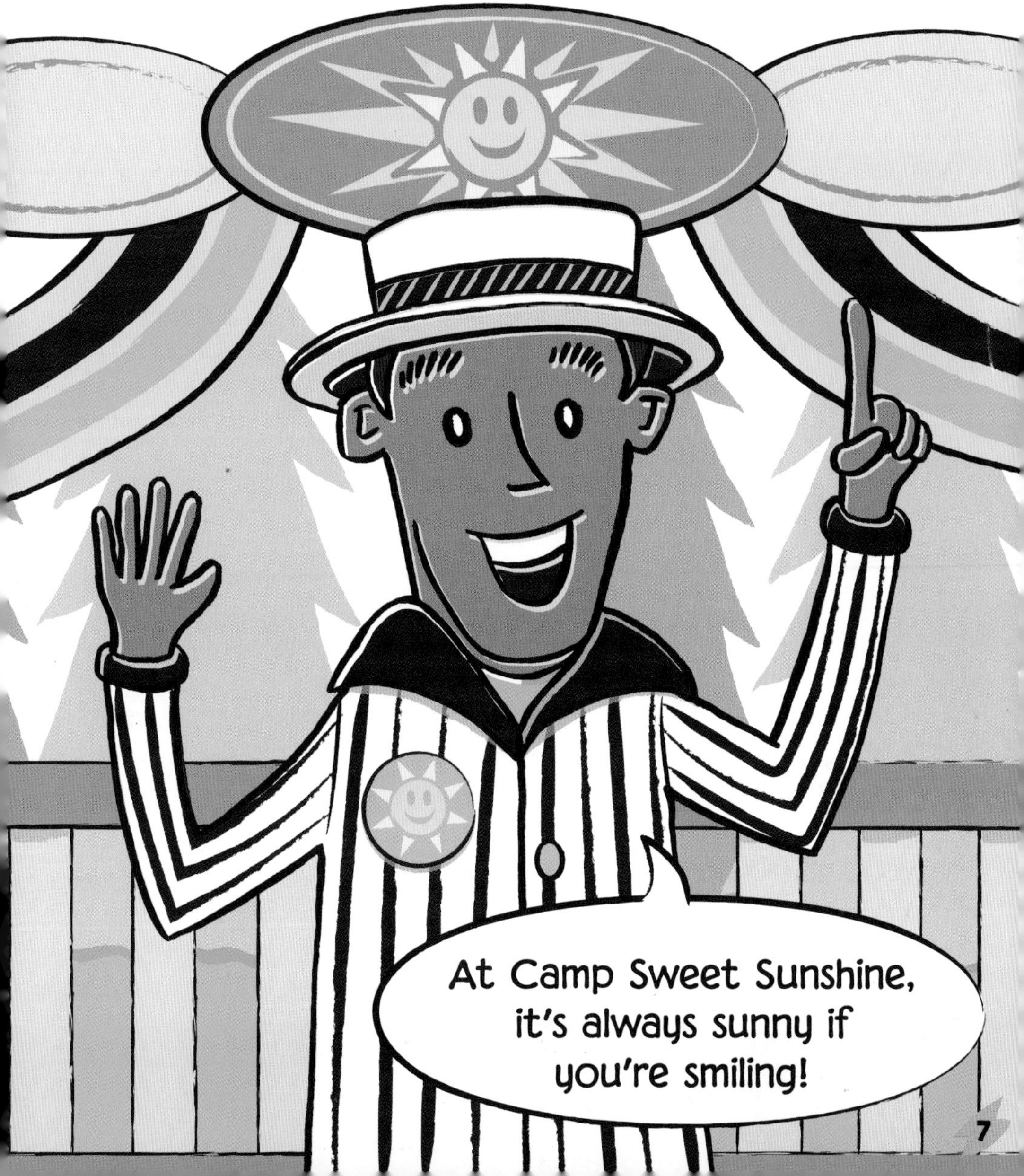
At Camp Sweet Sunshine, it's always sunny if you're smiling!

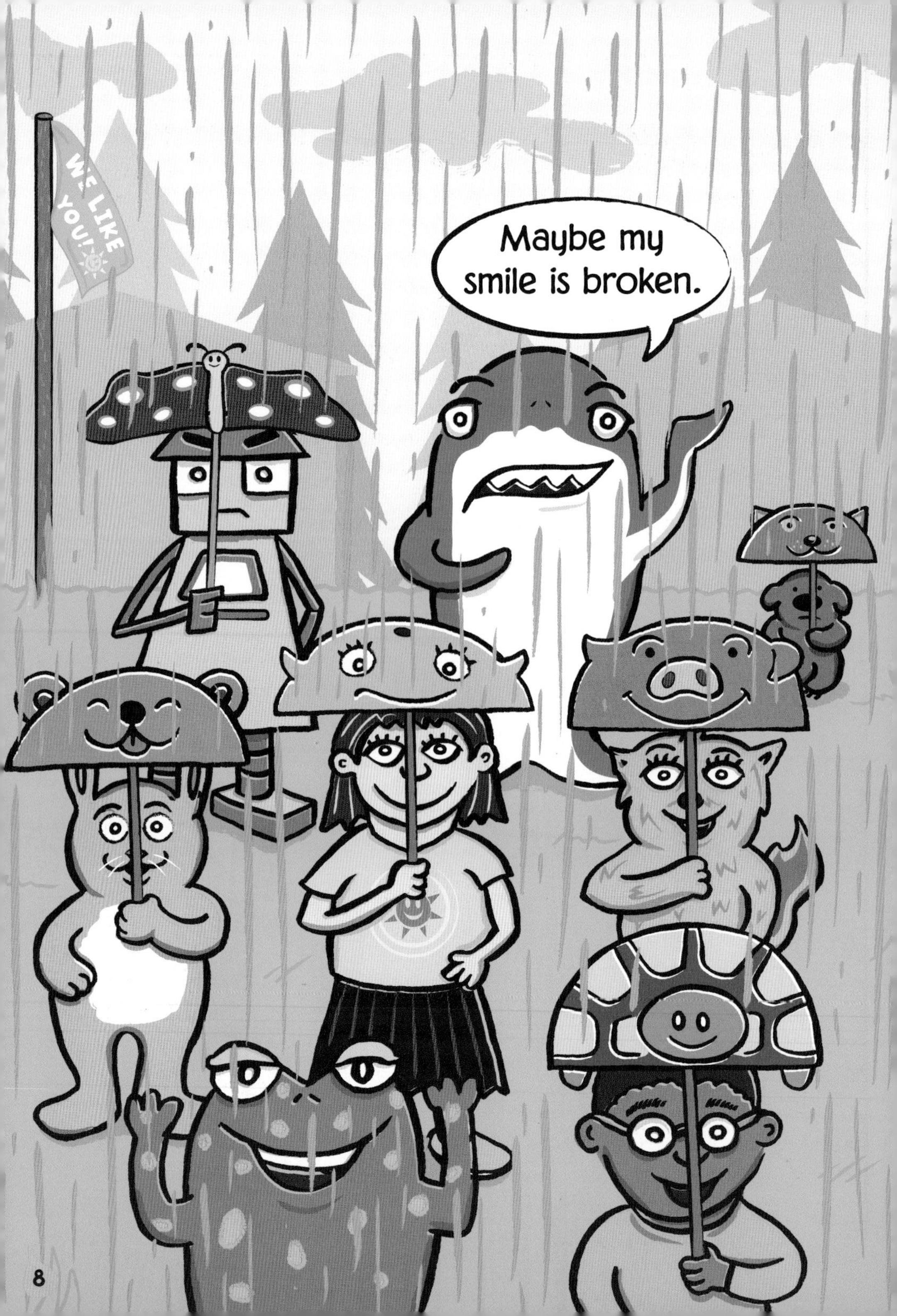
WE LIKE YOU!
Maybe my smile is broken.

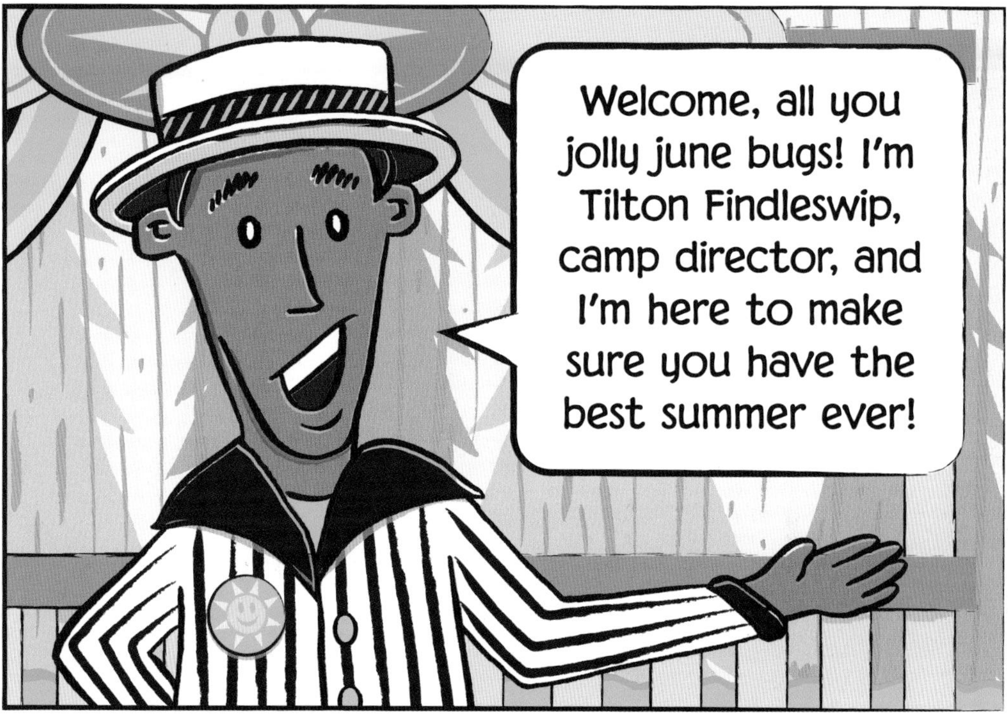
Welcome, all you jolly june bugs! I'm Tilton Findleswip, camp director, and I'm here to make sure you have the best summer ever!

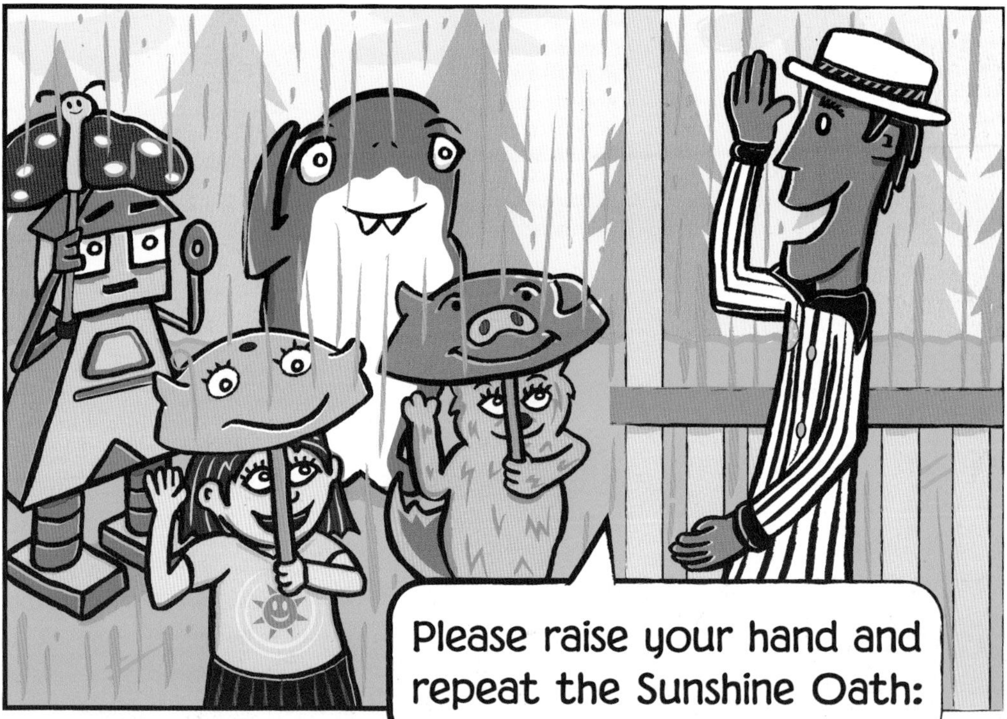
Please raise your hand and repeat the Sunshine Oath:

Sunshine Oath

I promise to...

1. Try new things.

2. Make new friends.

3. Do a good deed.

4. Make something beautiful.

5. Give free hugs.

With this oath, we will fill the world with giggles and glitter!

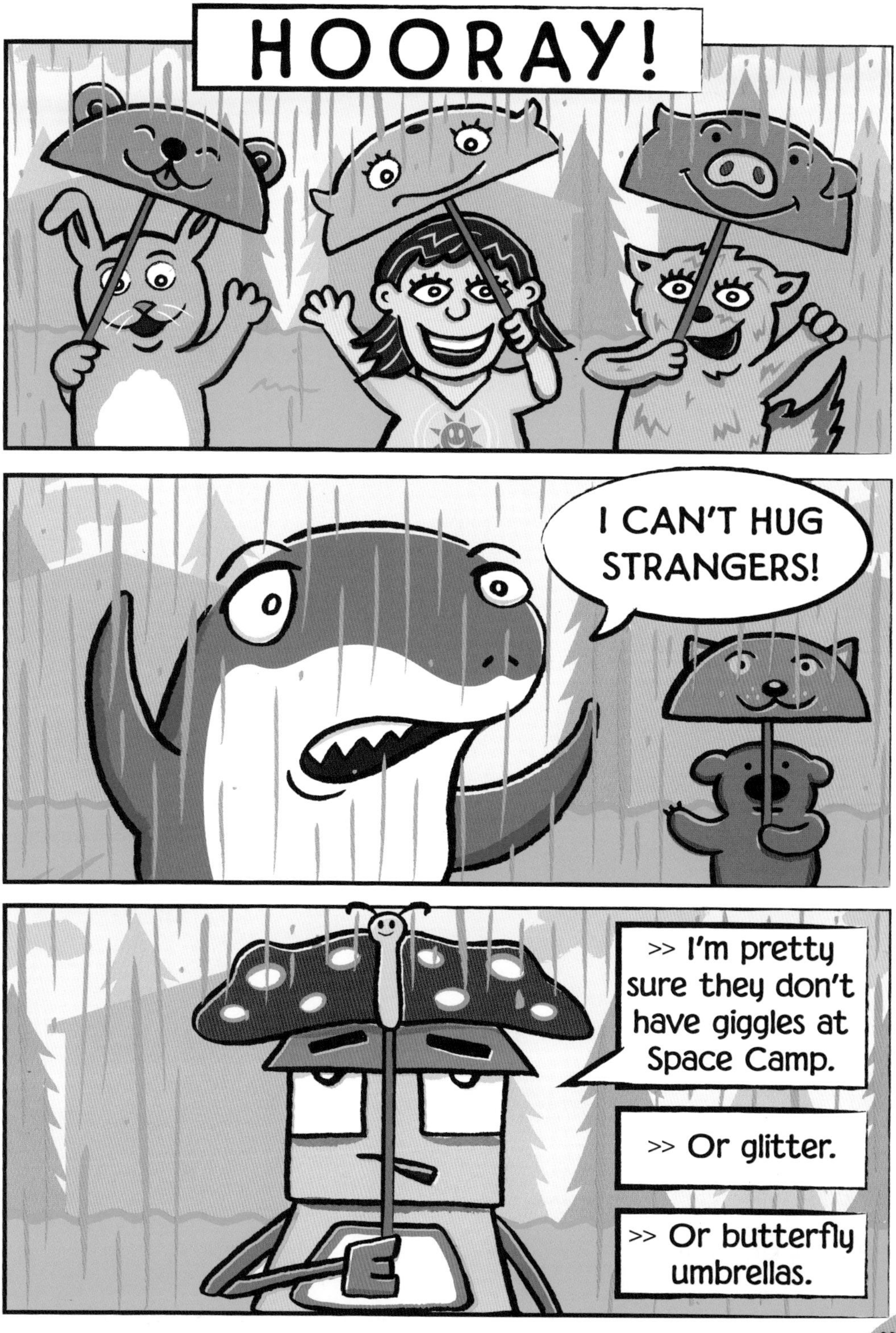

HOORAY!
I CAN'T HUG STRANGERS!
>> I'm pretty sure they don't have giggles at Space Camp.
>> Or glitter.
>> Or butterfly umbrellas.

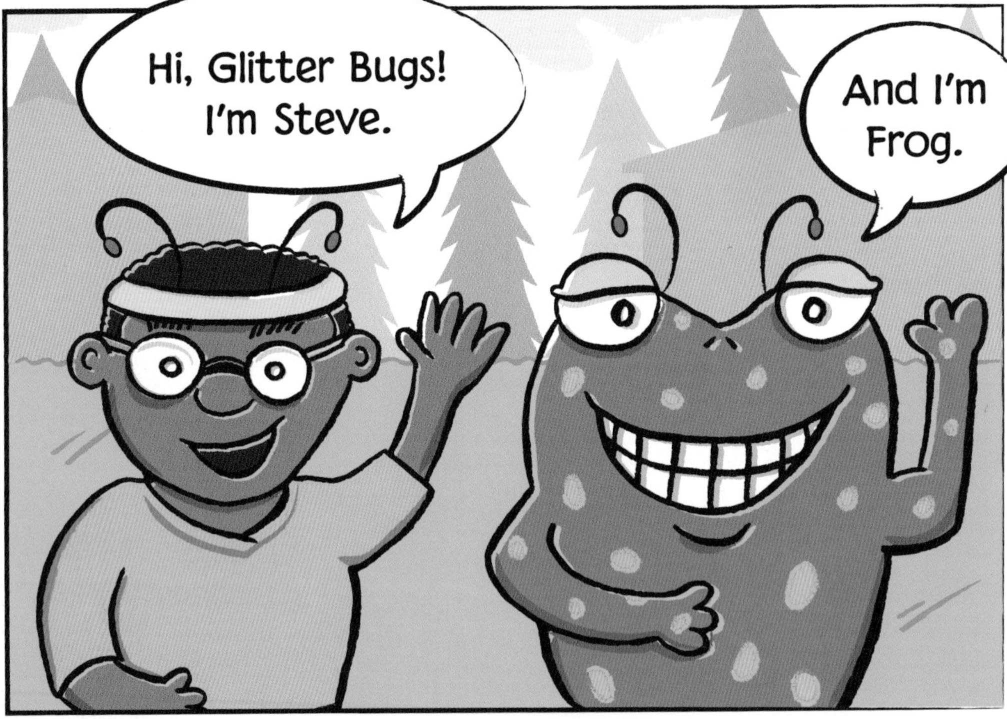
Hi, Glitter Bugs!
I'm Steve.
And I'm
Frog.

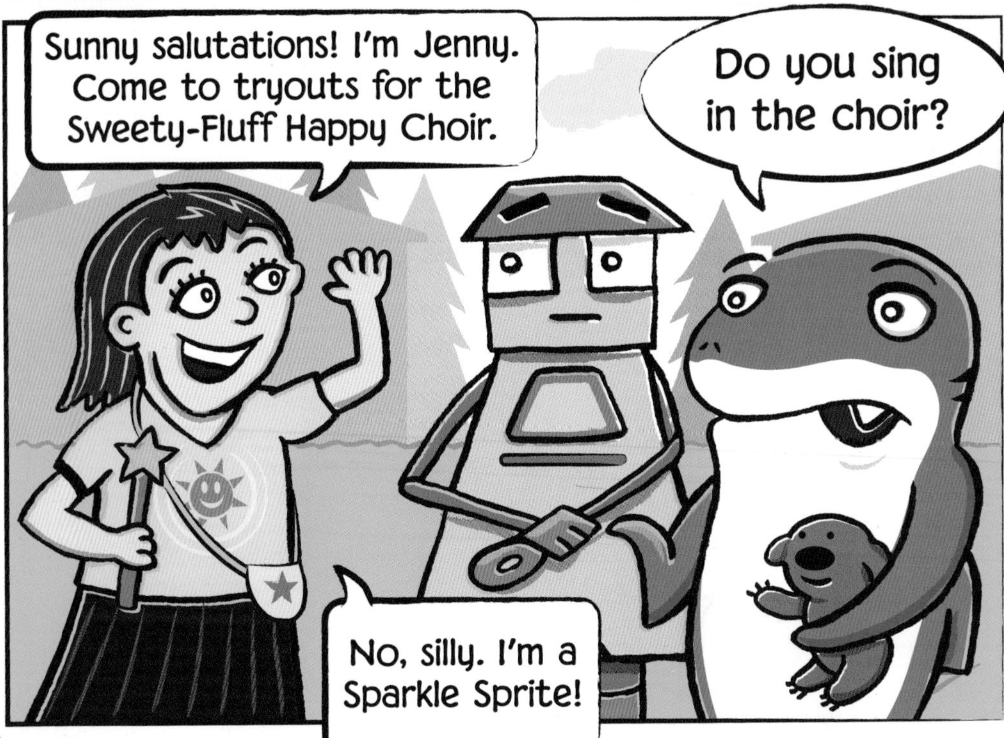
Sunny salutations! I'm Jenny.
Come to tryouts for the
Sweety-Fluff Happy Choir.
Do you sing
in the choir?
No, silly. I'm a
Sparkle Sprite!

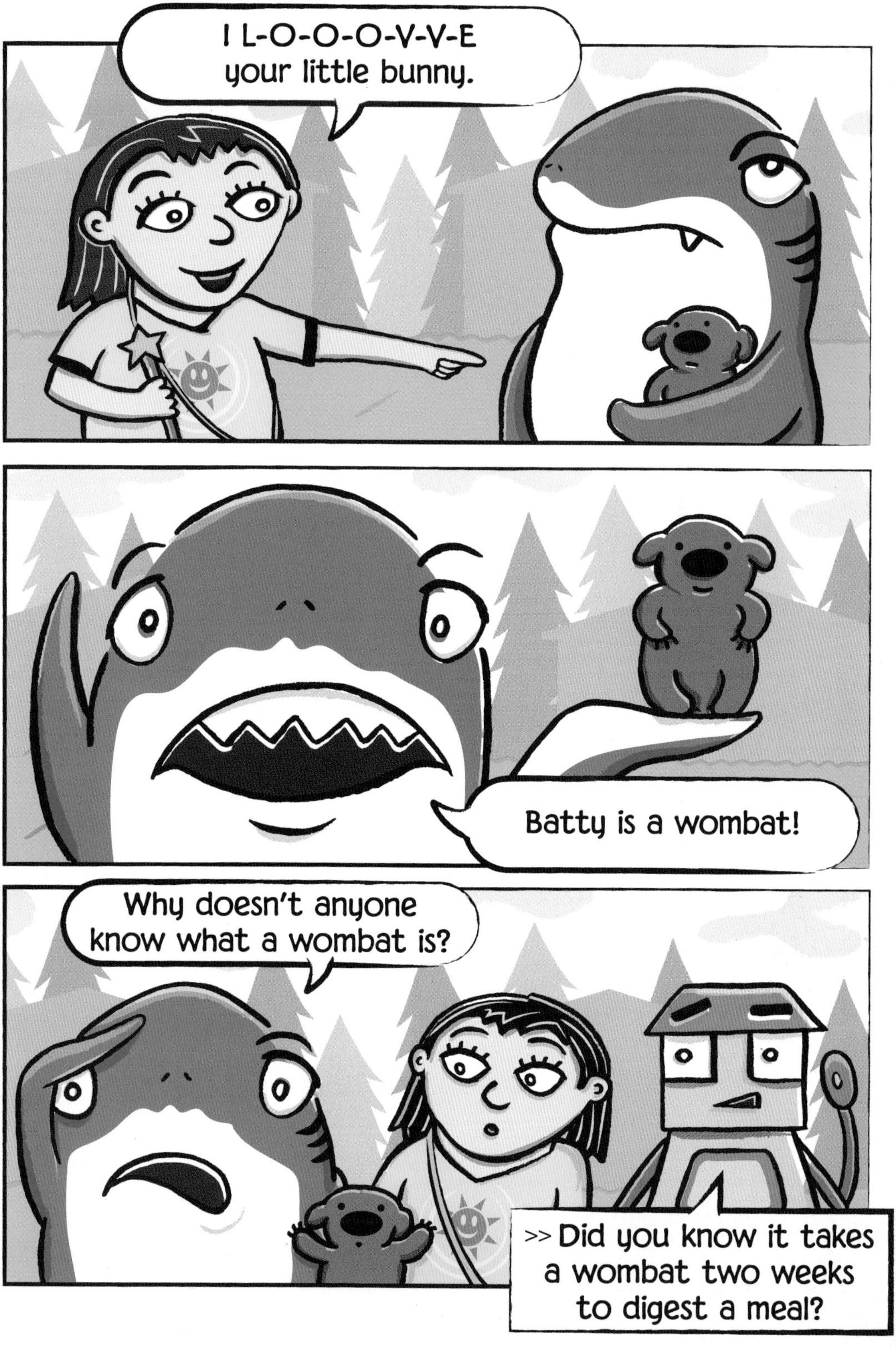
I L-O-O-O-V-V-E your little bunny.
Batty is a wombat!
Why doesn't anyone know what a wombat is?
>> Did you know it takes a wombat two weeks to digest a meal?

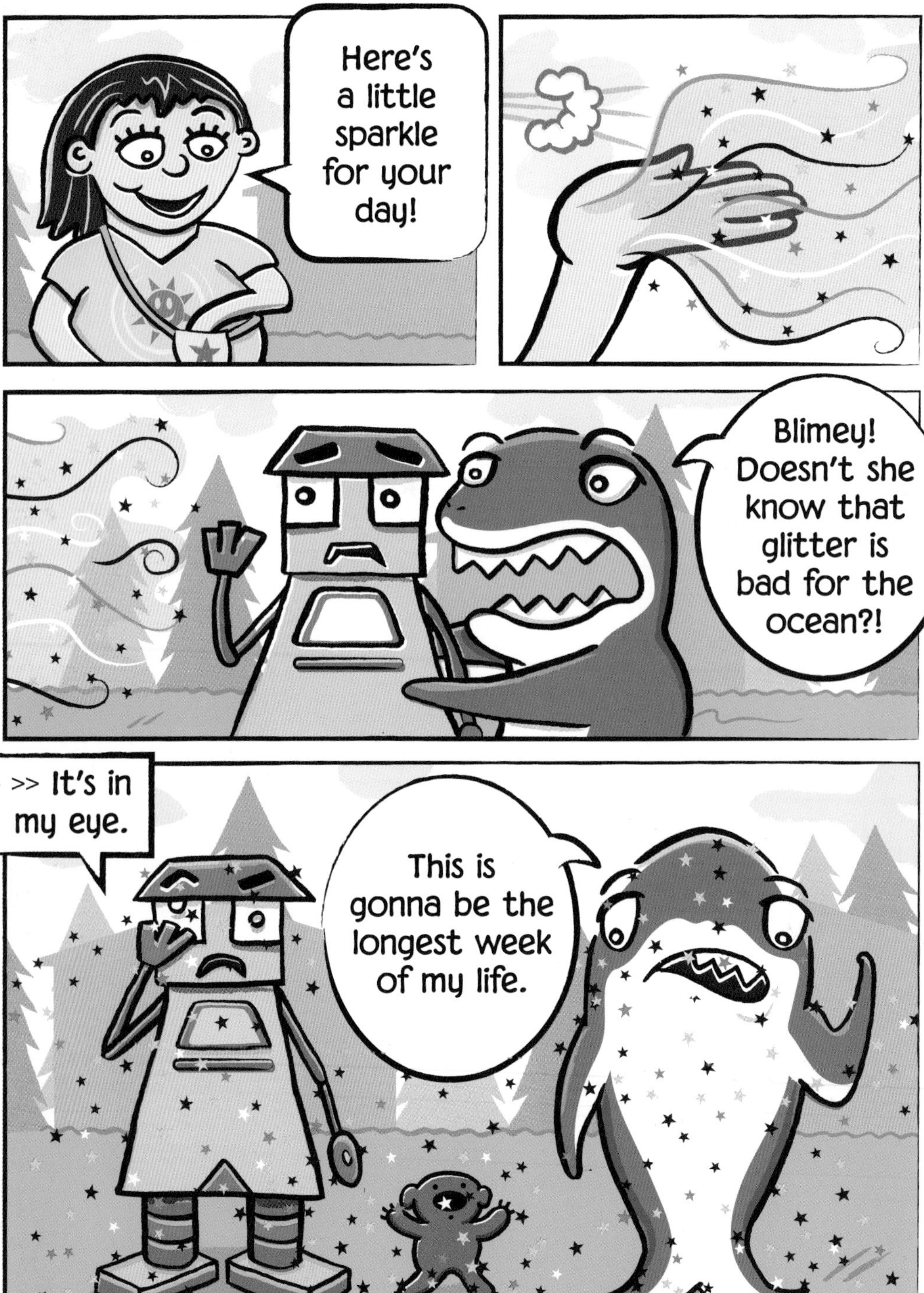
Here's a little sparkle for your day!
Blimey! Doesn't she know that glitter is bad for the ocean?!
>> It's in my eye.
This is gonna be the longest week of my life.

Chapter 3

Nightmares

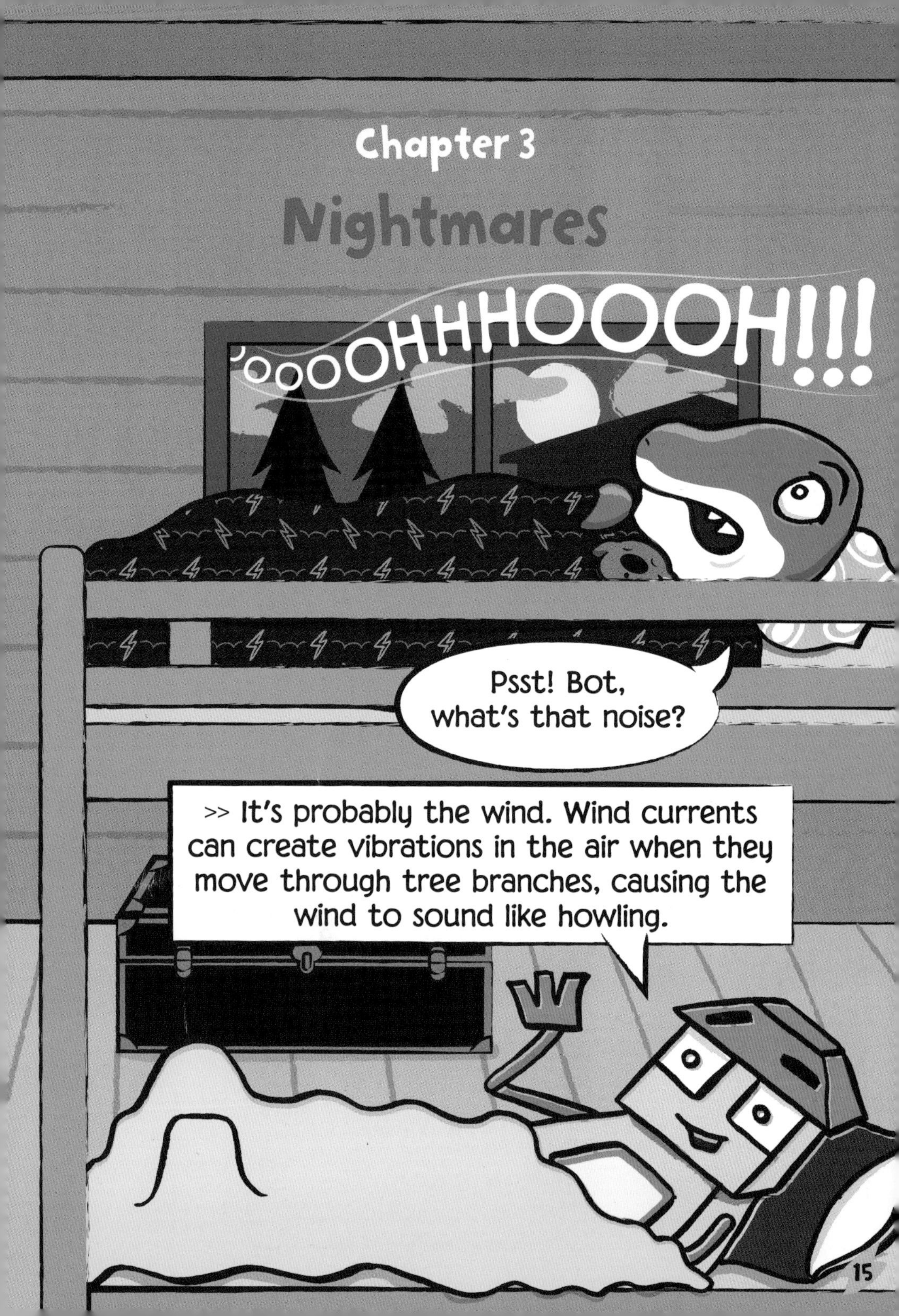

OOOOOHHHOOOOH!!!
Psst! Bot, what's that noise?
>> It's probably the wind. Wind currents can create vibrations in the air when they move through tree branches, causing the wind to sound like howling.

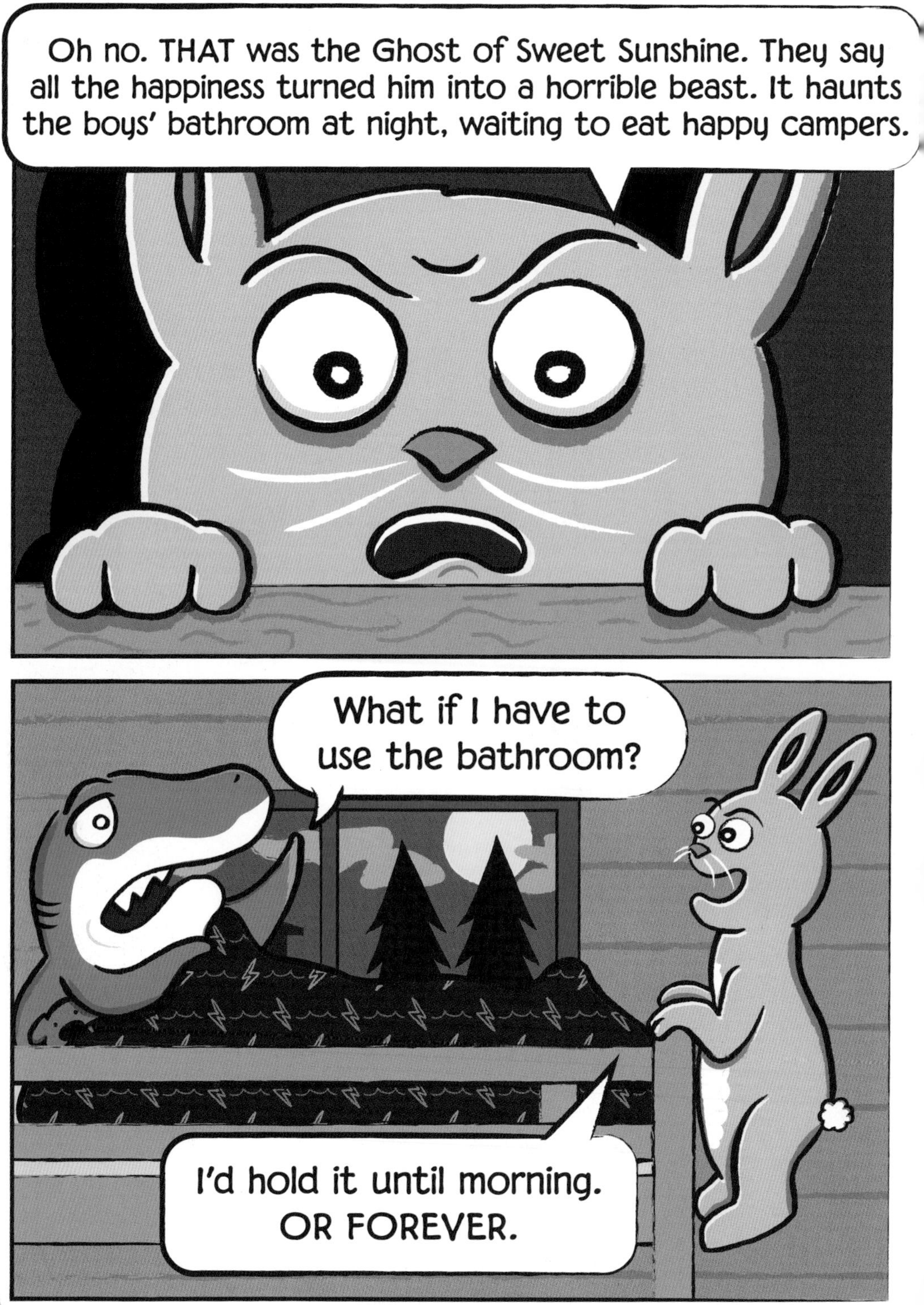
Oh no. THAT was the Ghost of Sweet Sunshine. They say all the happiness turned him into a horrible beast. It haunts the boys' bathroom at night, waiting to eat happy campers.
What if I have to use the bathroom?
I'd hold it until morning. OR FOREVER.

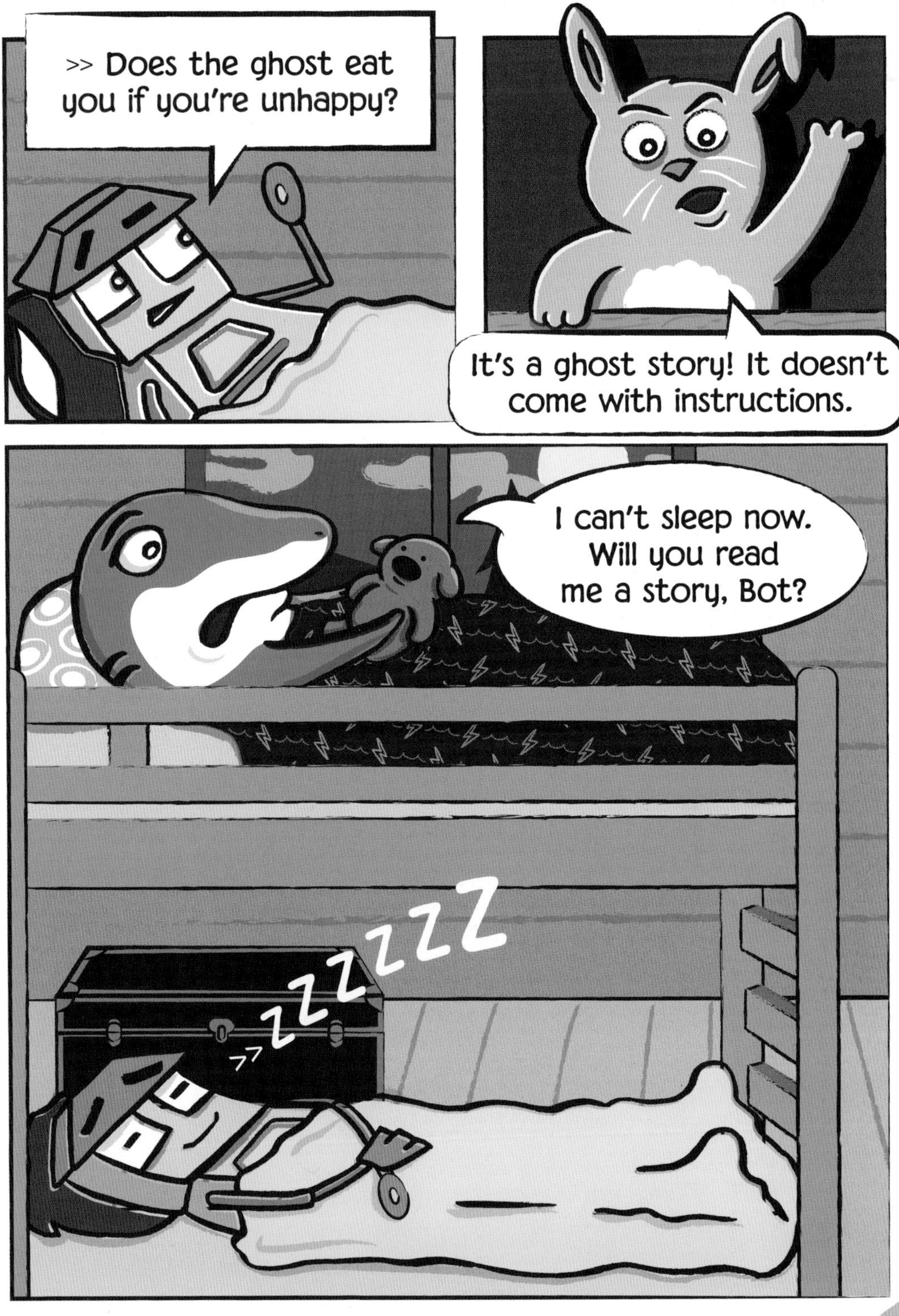
>> Does the ghost eat you if you're unhappy?
It's a ghost story! It doesn't come with instructions.
I can't sleep now. Will you read me a story, Bot?
>> ZZZZZZZ

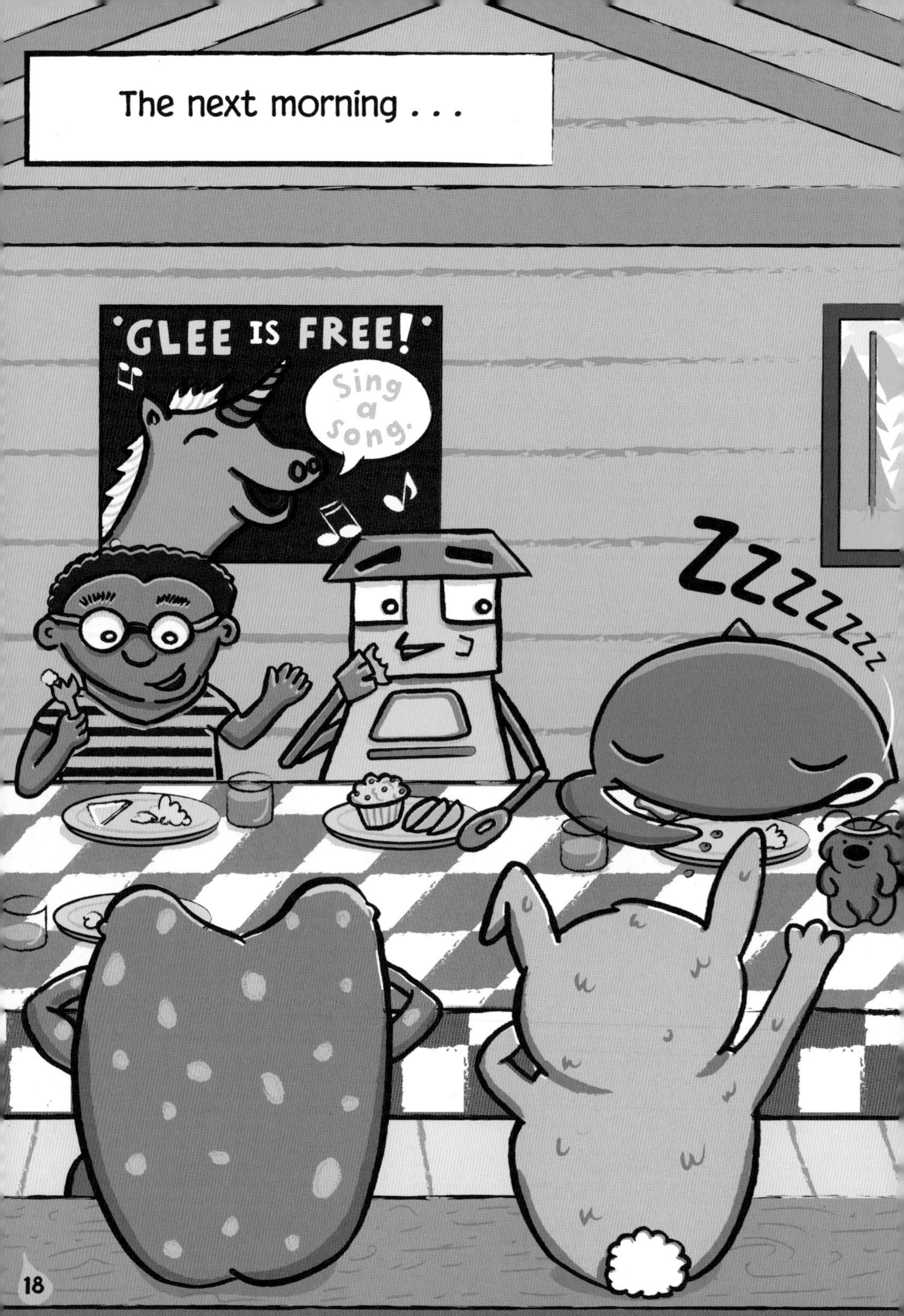
The next morning . . .
"GLEE IS FREE!"
Sing a song.
ZZZZZZZZZ

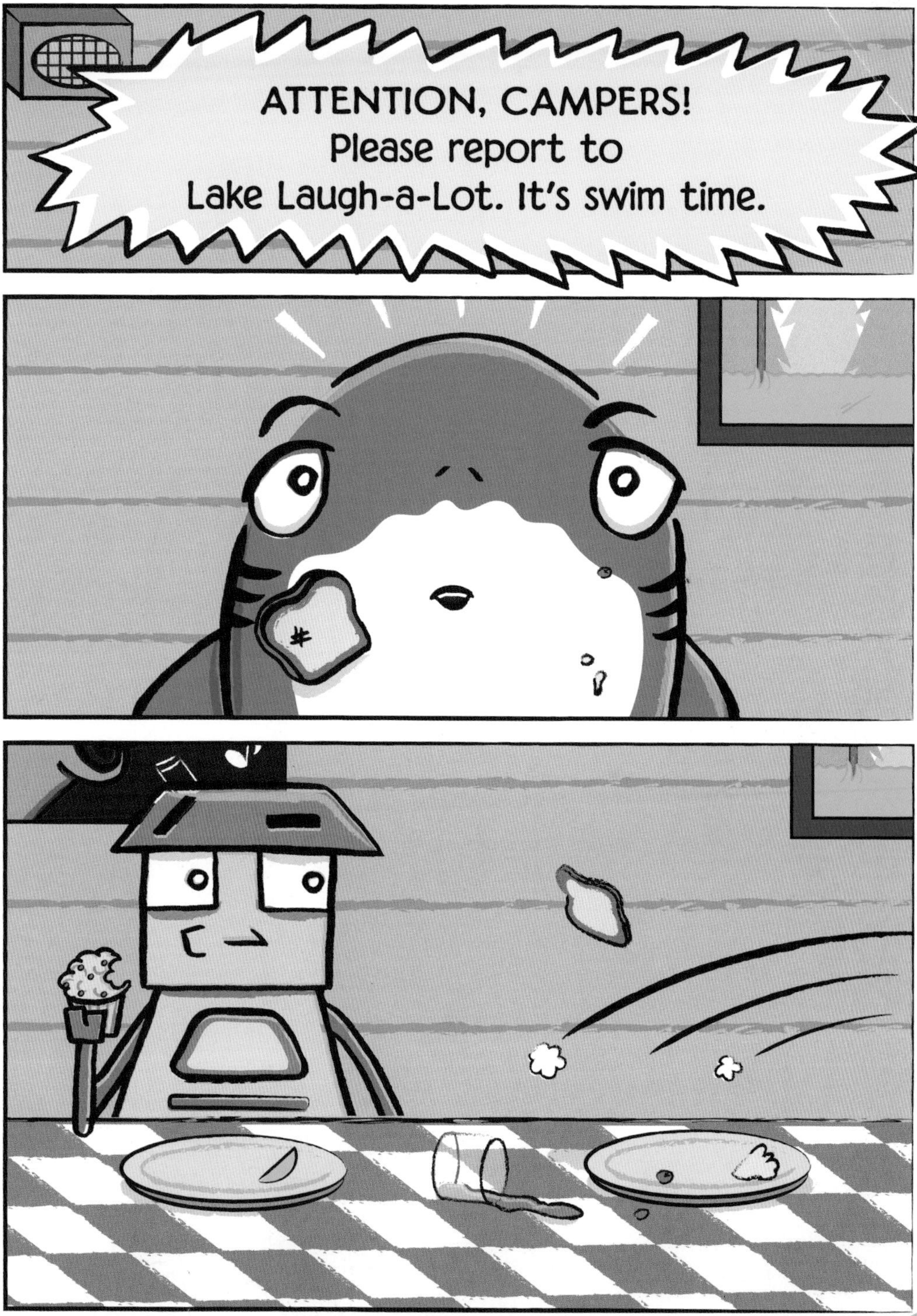
ATTENTION, CAMPERS! Please report to Lake Laugh-a-Lot. It's swim time.

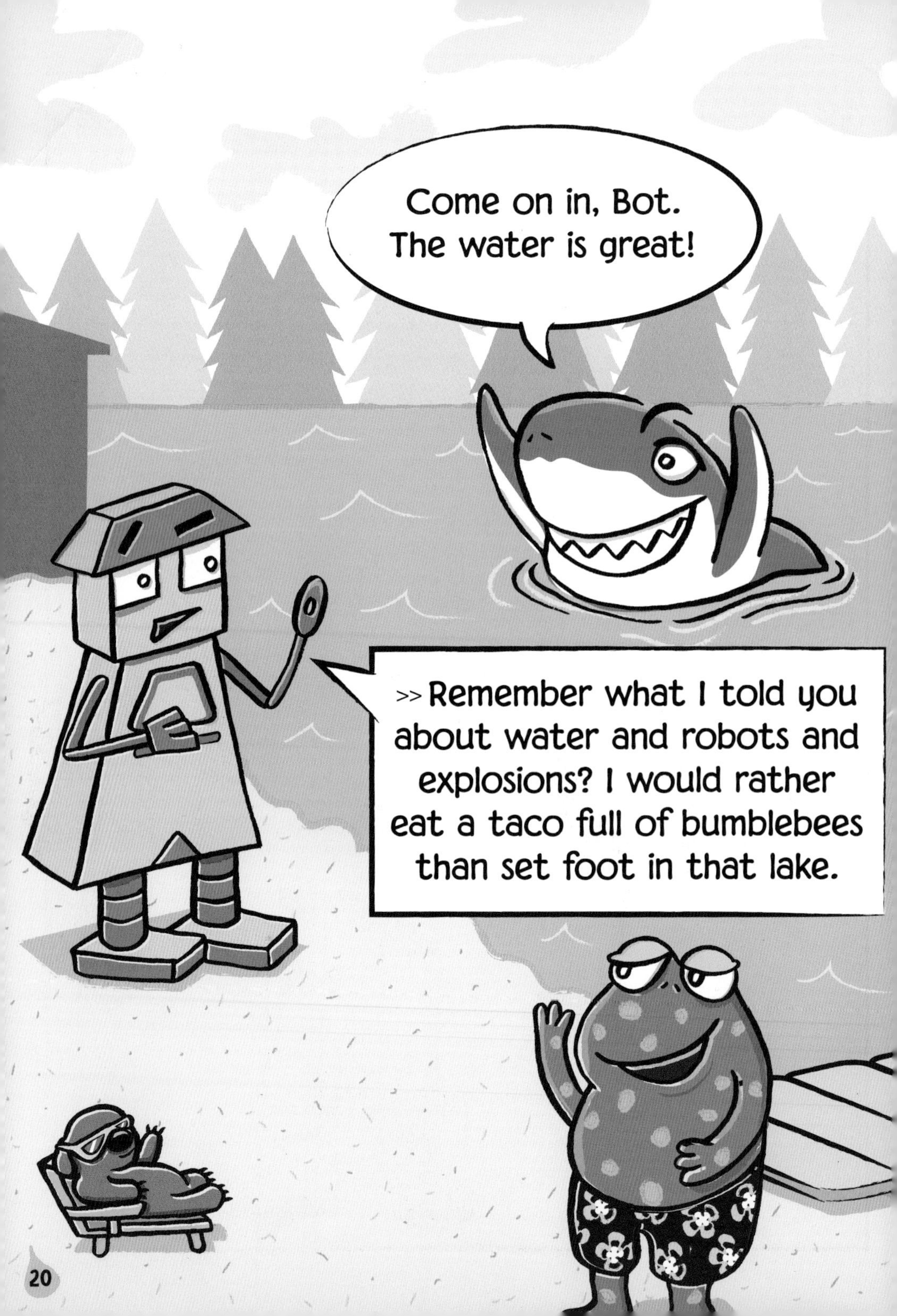
Come on in, Bot. The water is great!
>> Remember what I told you about water and robots and explosions? I would rather eat a taco full of bumblebees than set foot in that lake.

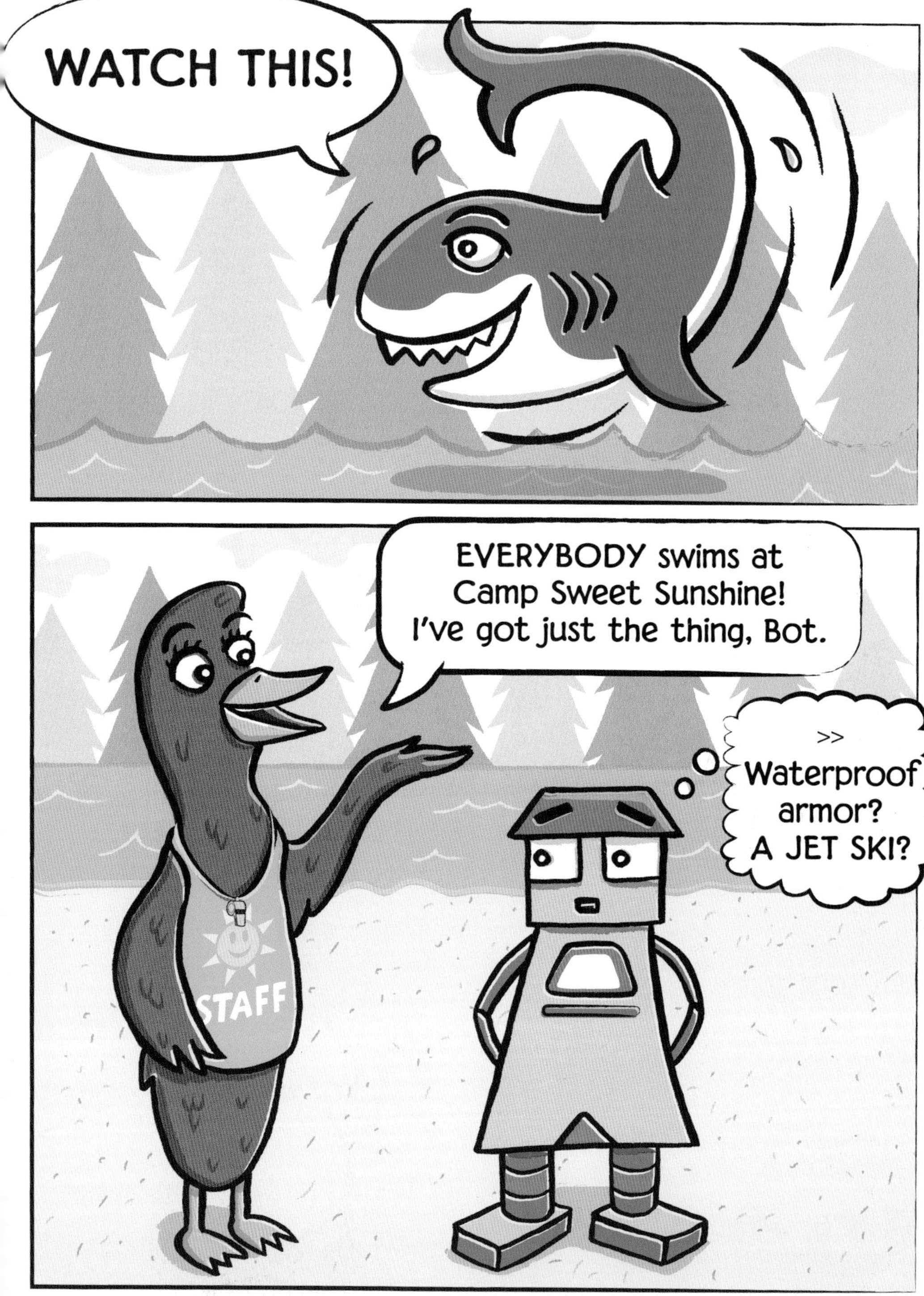
WATCH THIS!
EVERYBODY swims at Camp Sweet Sunshine! I've got just the thing, Bot.
STAFF
>> Waterproof armor? A JET SKI?

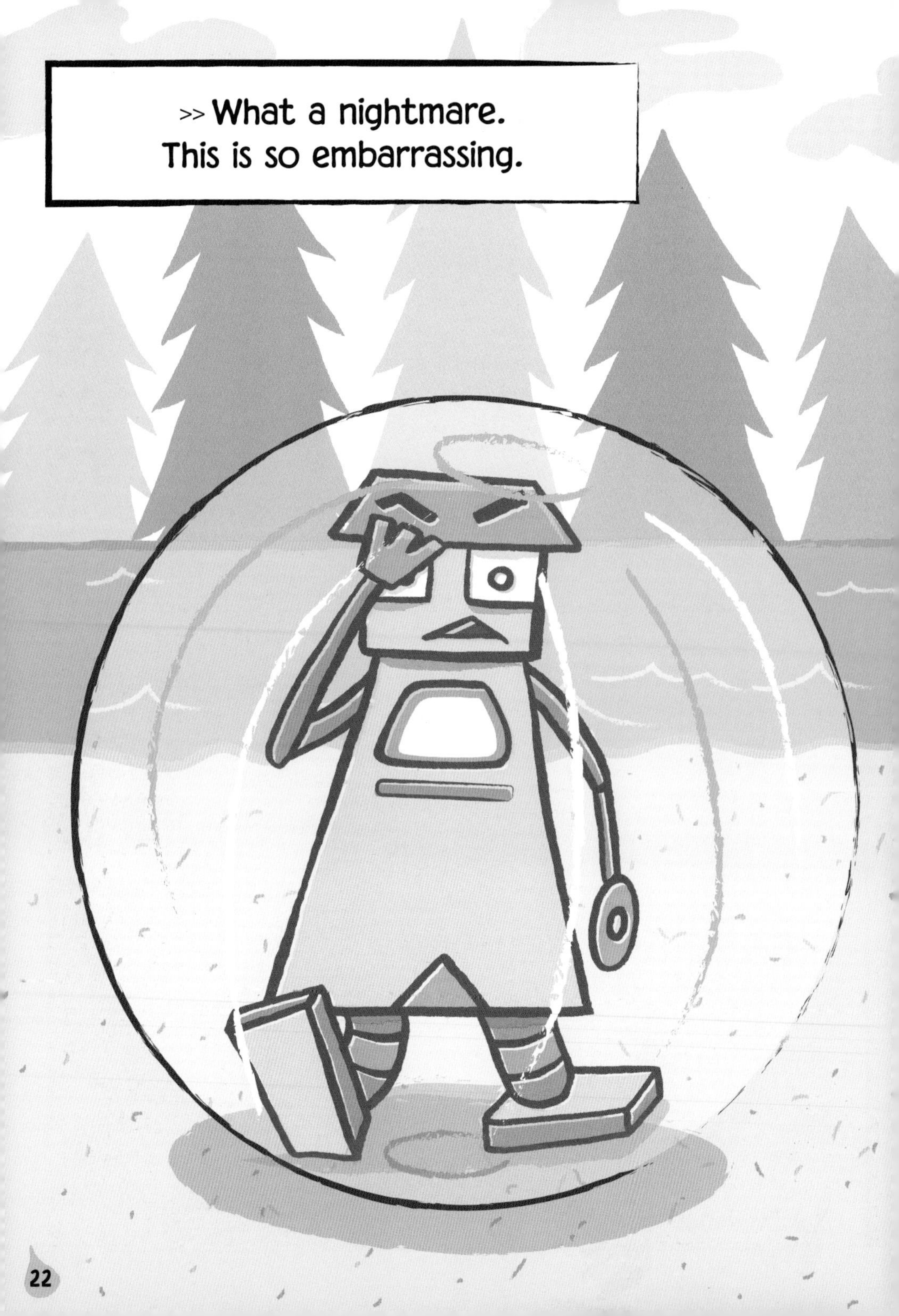
>> What a nightmare.
This is so embarrassing.

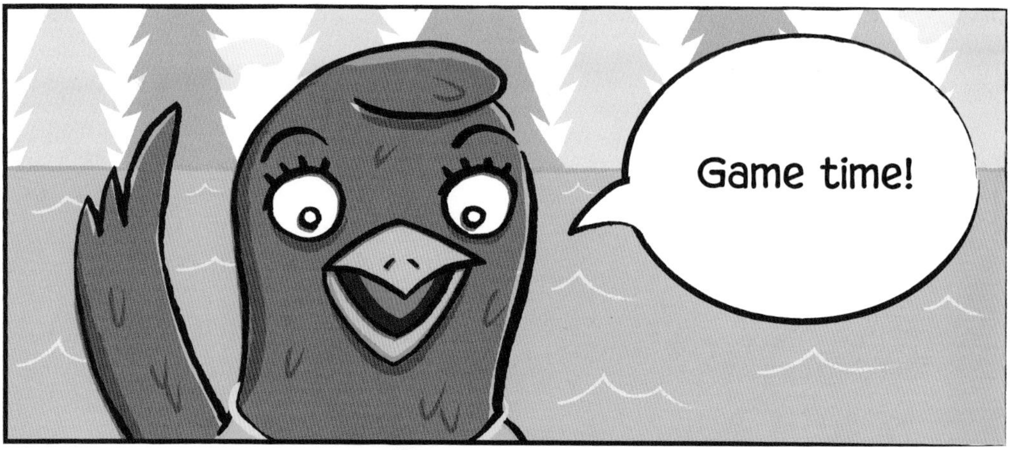
Game time!

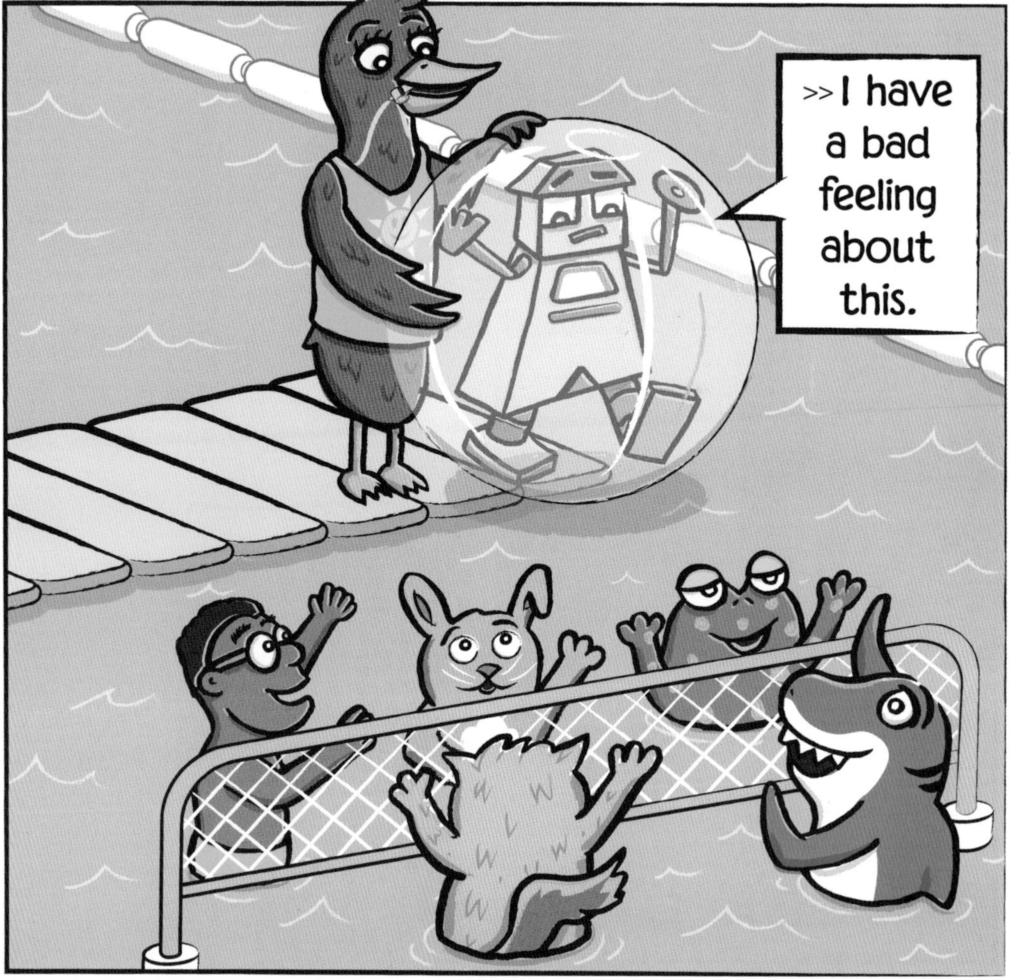
>>I have a bad feeling about this.

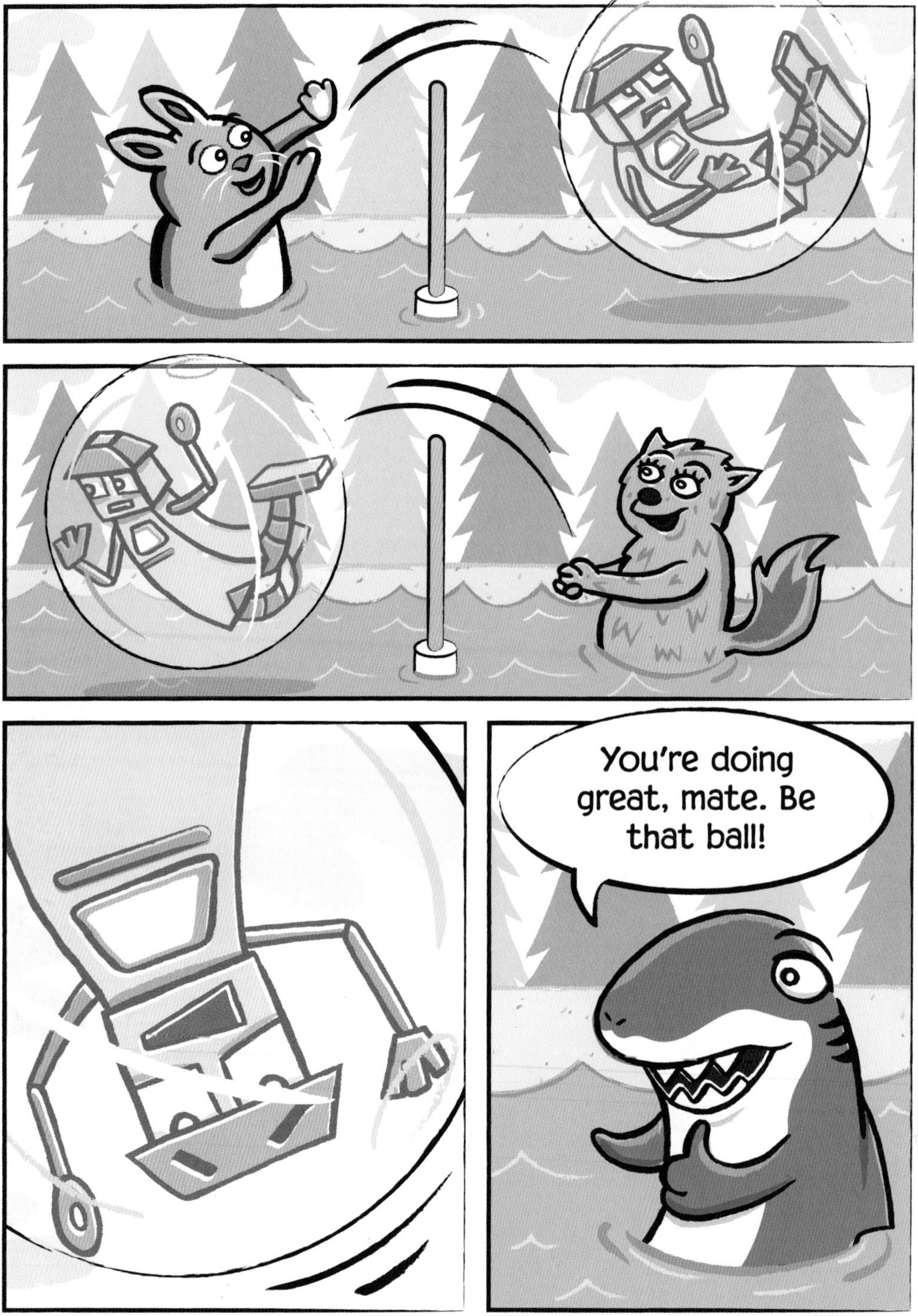
You're doing great, mate. Be that ball!

We make the world feel special,
each flower, bear, and bug-snakes too!
With lots of sunny sparkles
and lots of loving hugs.

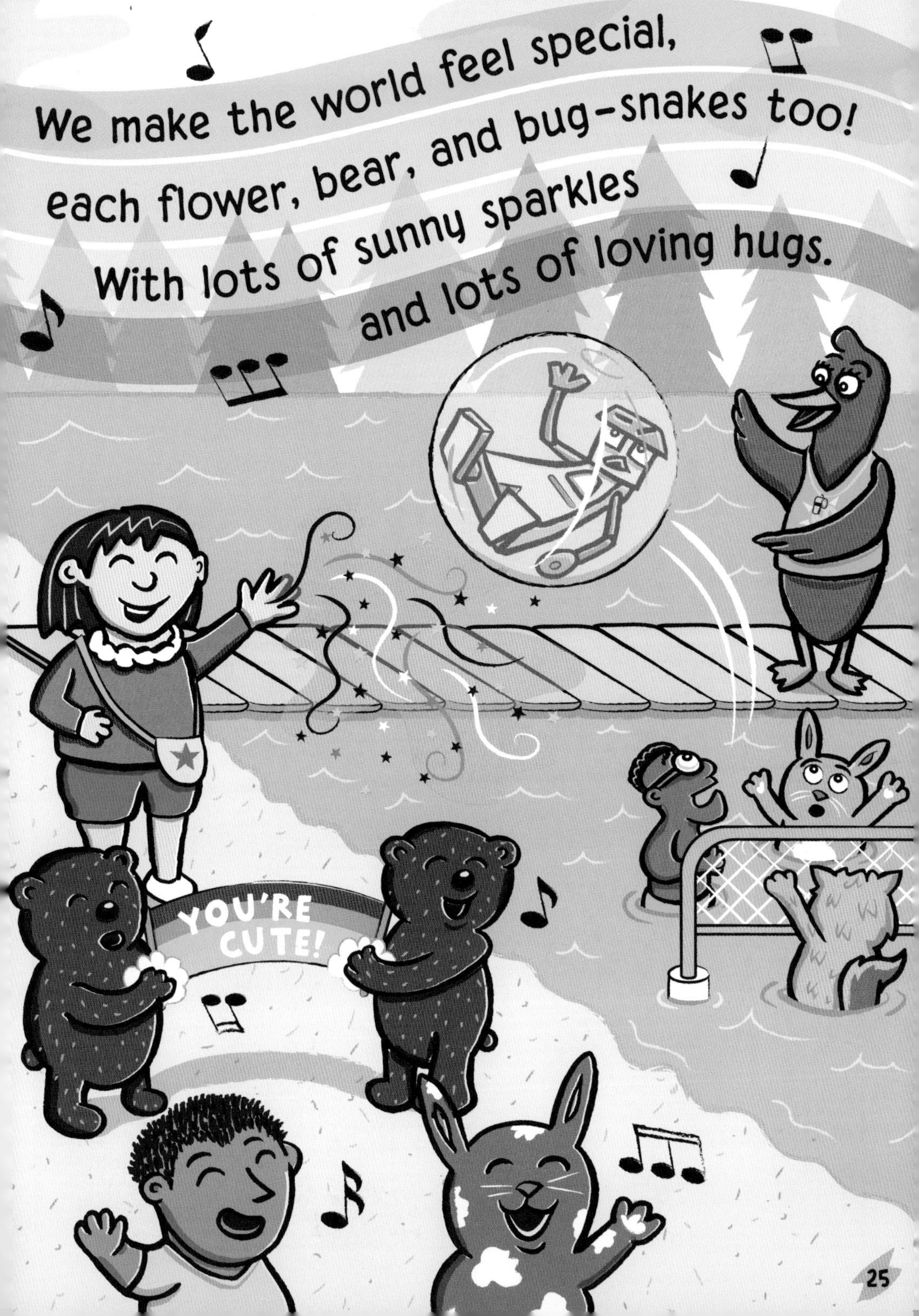
YOU'RE CUTE!

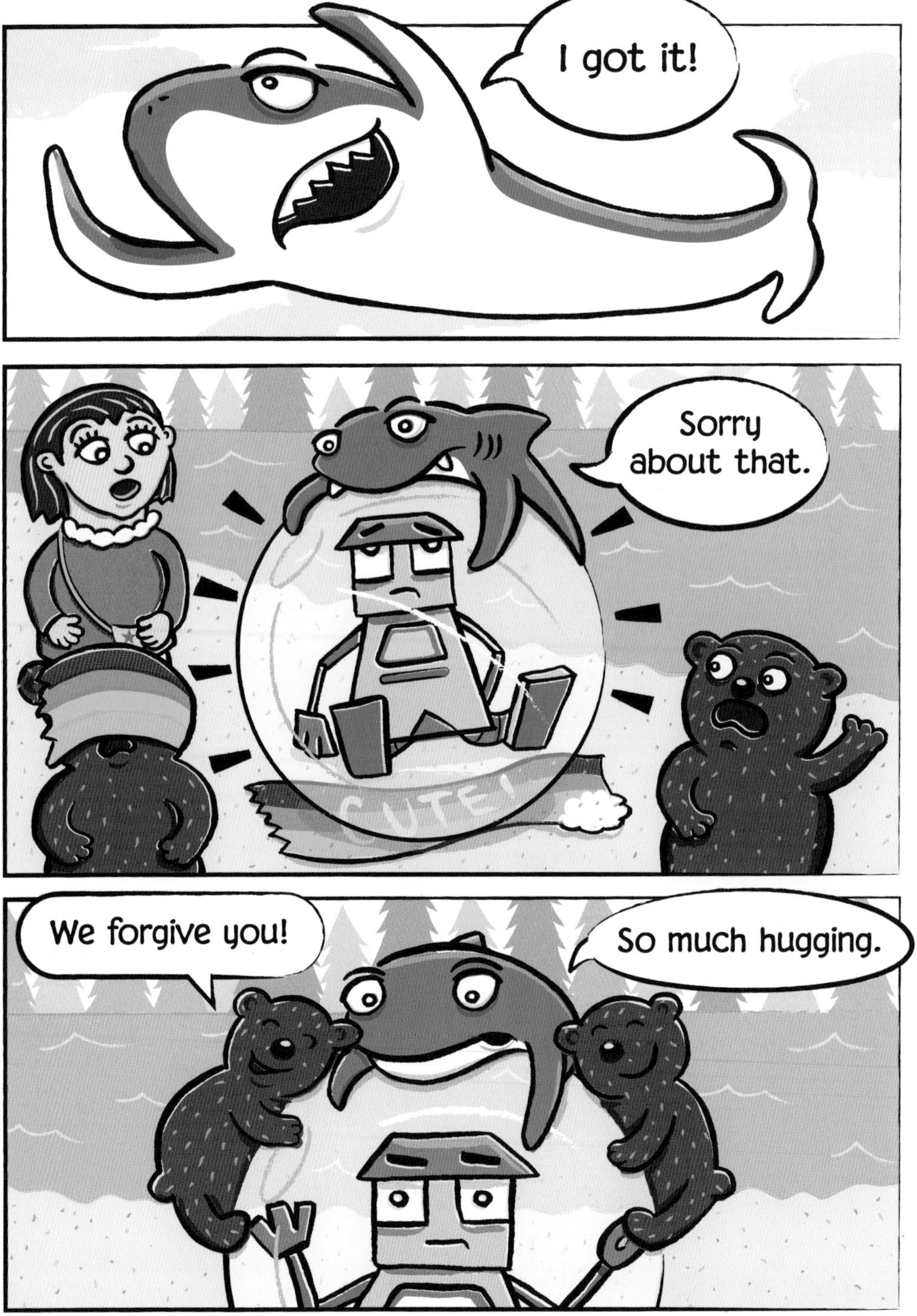
I got it!
Sorry about that.
CUTE!
We forgive you!
So much hugging.

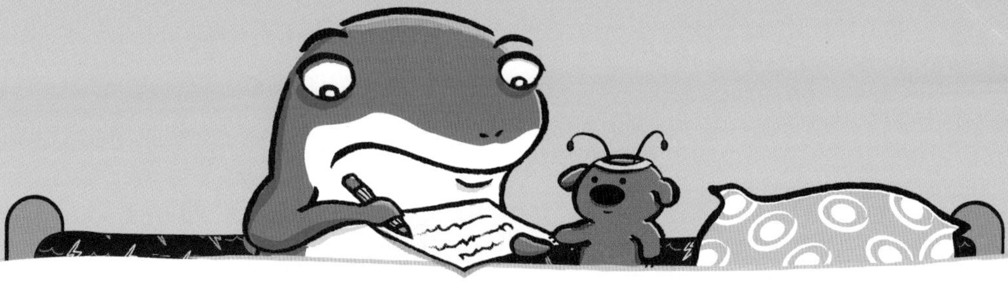

Dear Mom and Dad,

Camp Sweet Sunshine is full of clouds. I swam in the lake. That was fun for a while. The cabins are comfy but I haven't slept in 3 days. ~~We~~ I can't go to the bathroom because a ghost lives there.

I am a Glitter Bug. → 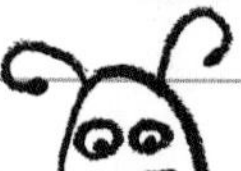

So is Bot. Otherwise, life is great.

Please send a car
to get me immediately.

Love + Fins,

SHARK

Chapter 4

Getting Crafty

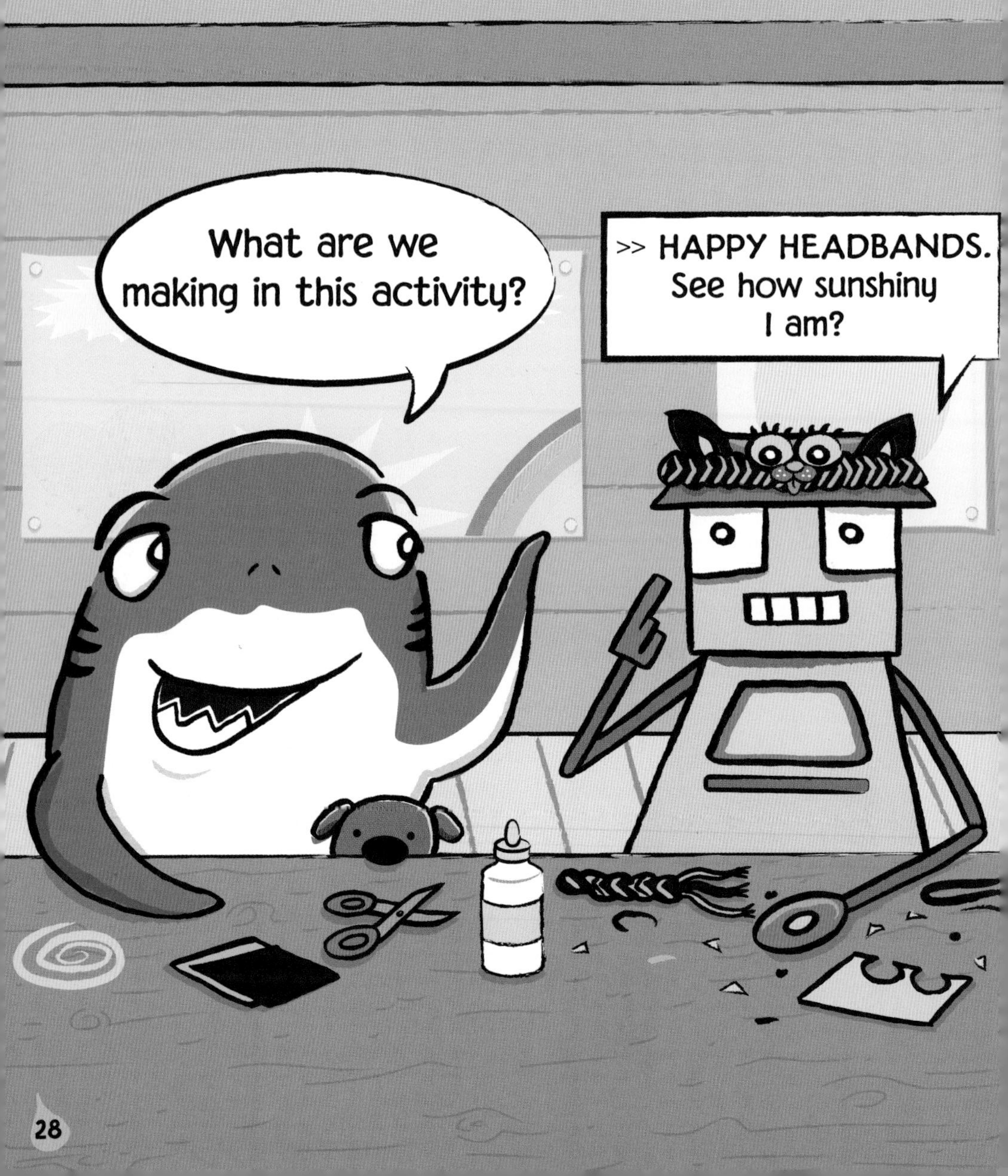
What are we making in this activity?
>> HAPPY HEADBANDS. See how sunshiny I am?

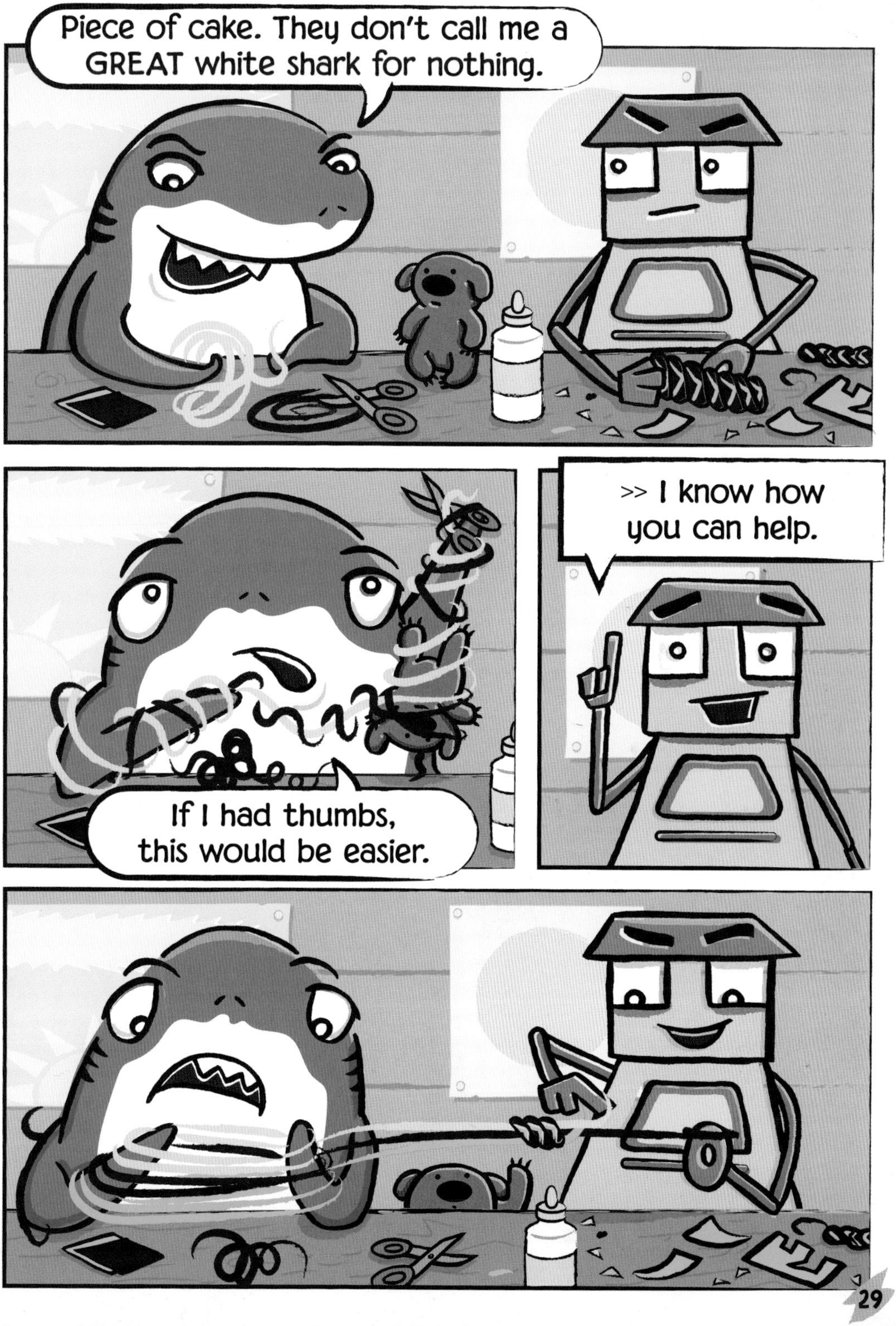
Piece of cake. They don't call me a GREAT white shark for nothing.
If I had thumbs, this would be easier.
>> I know how you can help.

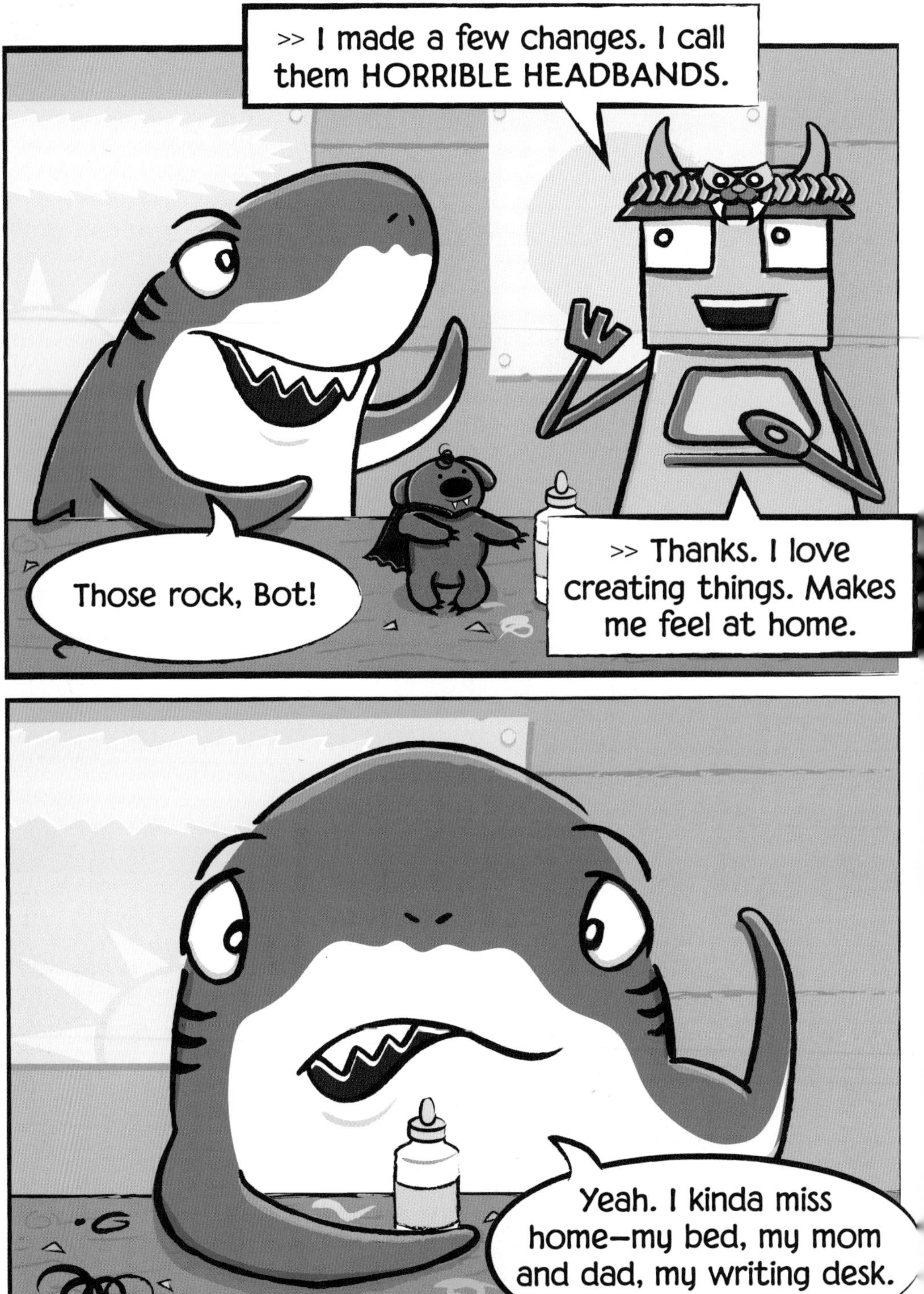

>> I made a few changes. I call them HORRIBLE HEADBANDS.
Those rock, Bot!
>> Thanks. I love creating things. Makes me feel at home.
Yeah. I kinda miss home—my bed, my mom and dad, my writing desk.

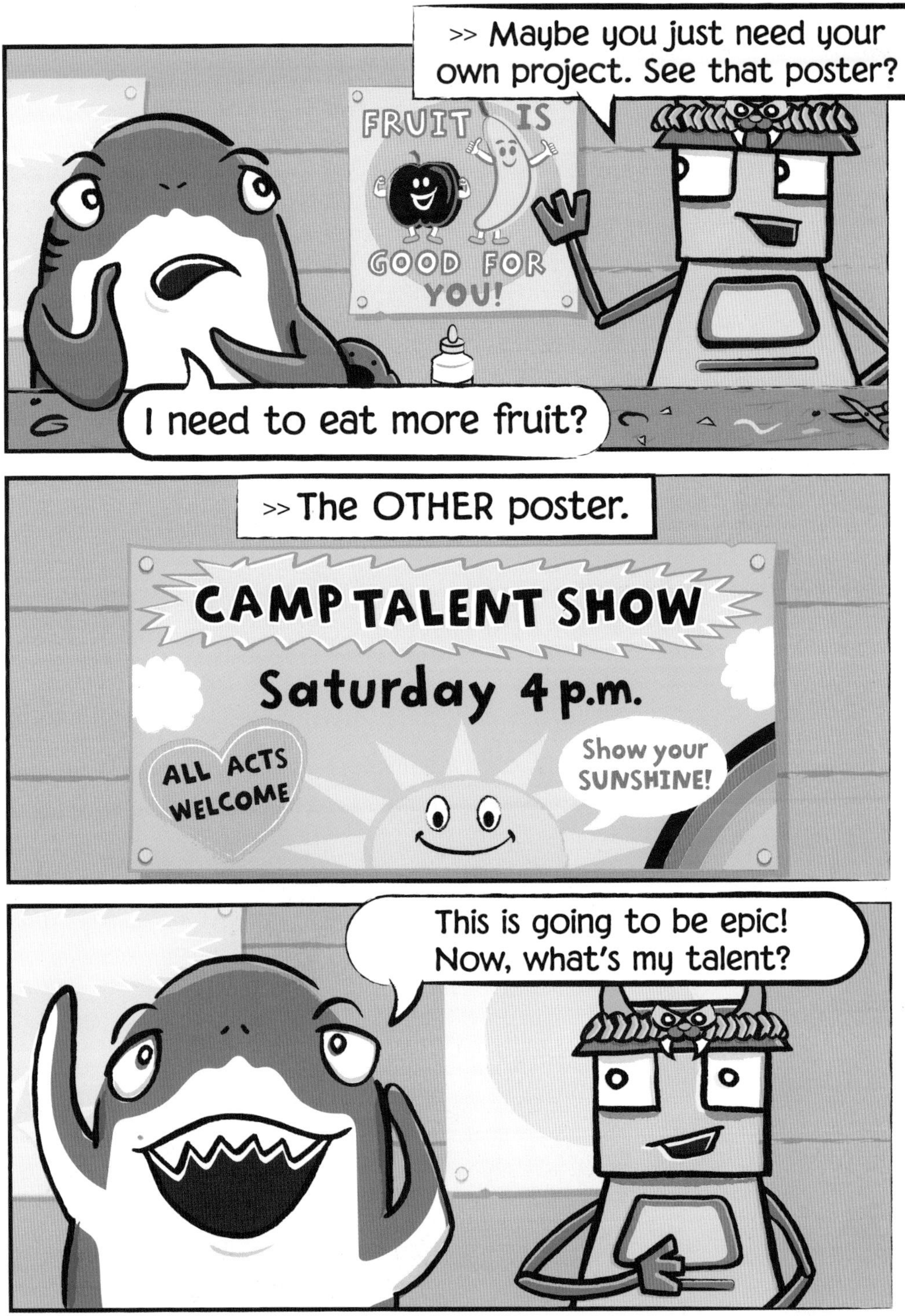
>> Maybe you just need your own project. See that poster?
FRUIT IS GOOD FOR YOU!
I need to eat more fruit?
>> The OTHER poster.
CAMP TALENT SHOW
Saturday 4 p.m.
ALL ACTS WELCOME
Show your SUNSHINE!
This is going to be epic! Now, what's my talent?

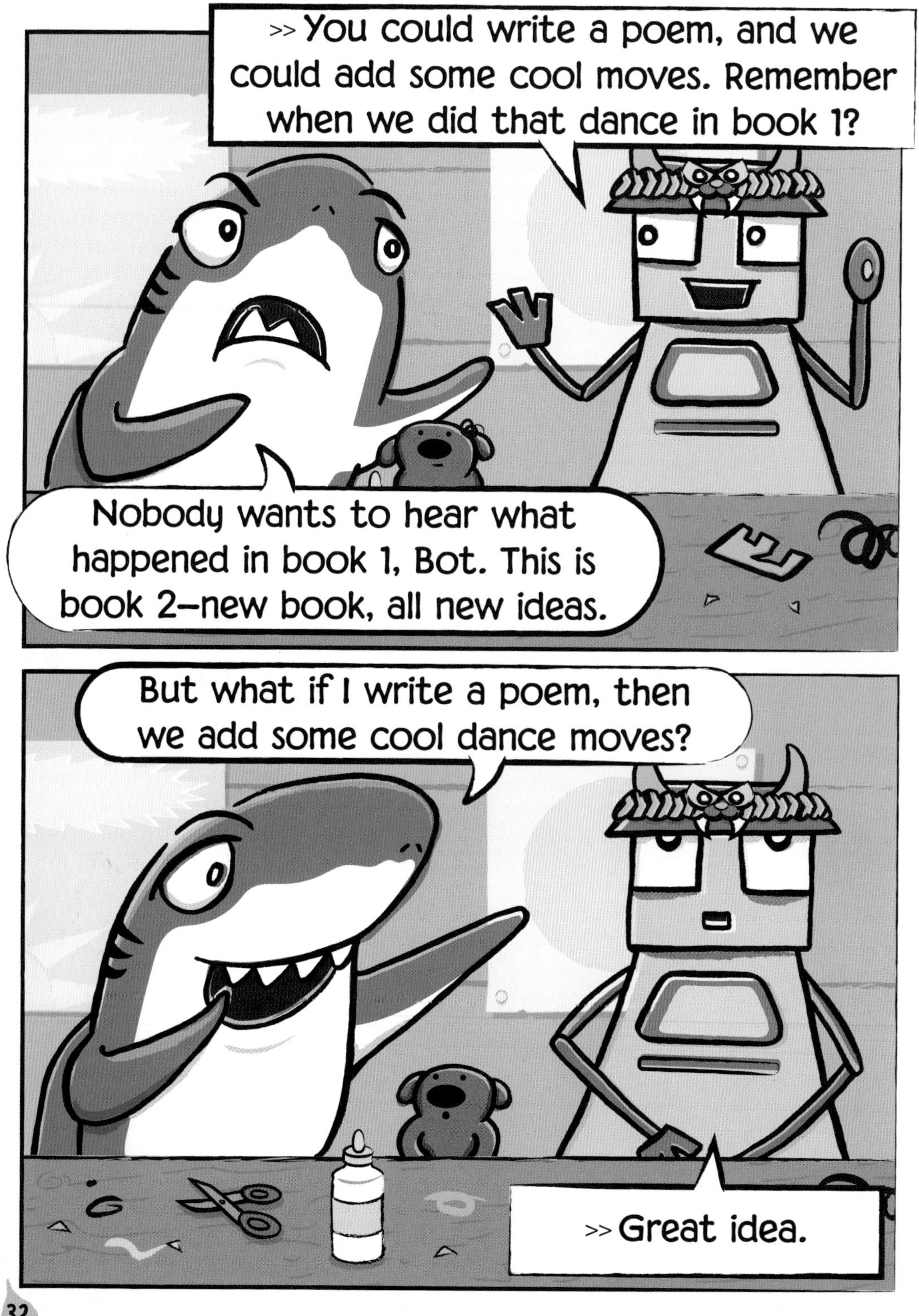
>> You could write a poem, and we could add some cool moves. Remember when we did that dance in book 1?
Nobody wants to hear what happened in book 1, Bot. This is book 2—new book, all new ideas.
But what if I write a poem, then we add some cool dance moves?
>> Great idea.

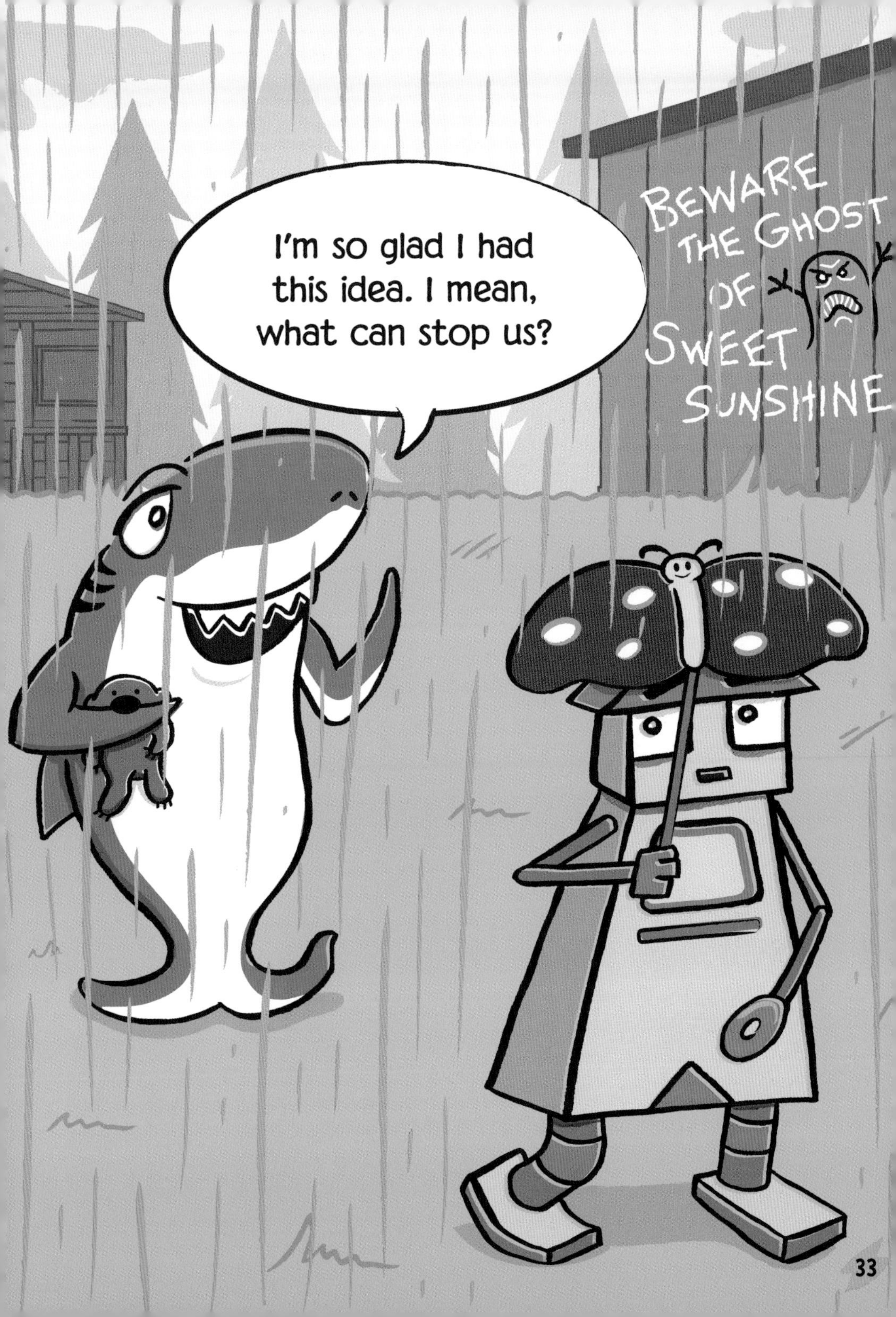
I'm so glad I had this idea. I mean, what can stop us?
BEWARE THE GHOST OF SWEET SUNSHINE

****

TO: MOM + DAD + ROBY

This is Bot. I am at camp.

SOME FACTS:

1. I made some really cool crafts.
2. Shark, Frog, Steve + Rabbit are in my cabin.
3. This is NOT Space Camp.
4. It rains every 112 minutes here.
5. I went swimming. Do not worry. I am still alive. Who else would be writing this letter?
6. I got glitter in my eye.
7. Shark is getting on my nerves, but he is still my best friend.
8. I ate pancakes.

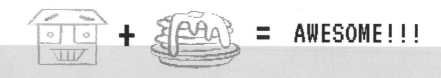

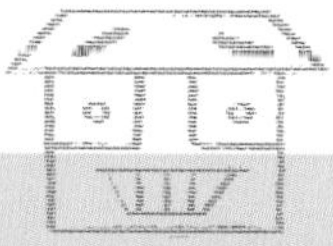 + 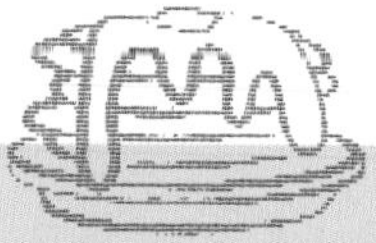 = AWESOME!!!

Tell Roby hi, and NOT to go in my room!

Beep beep, **BOT**

****

Chapter 5

What Did You Get?

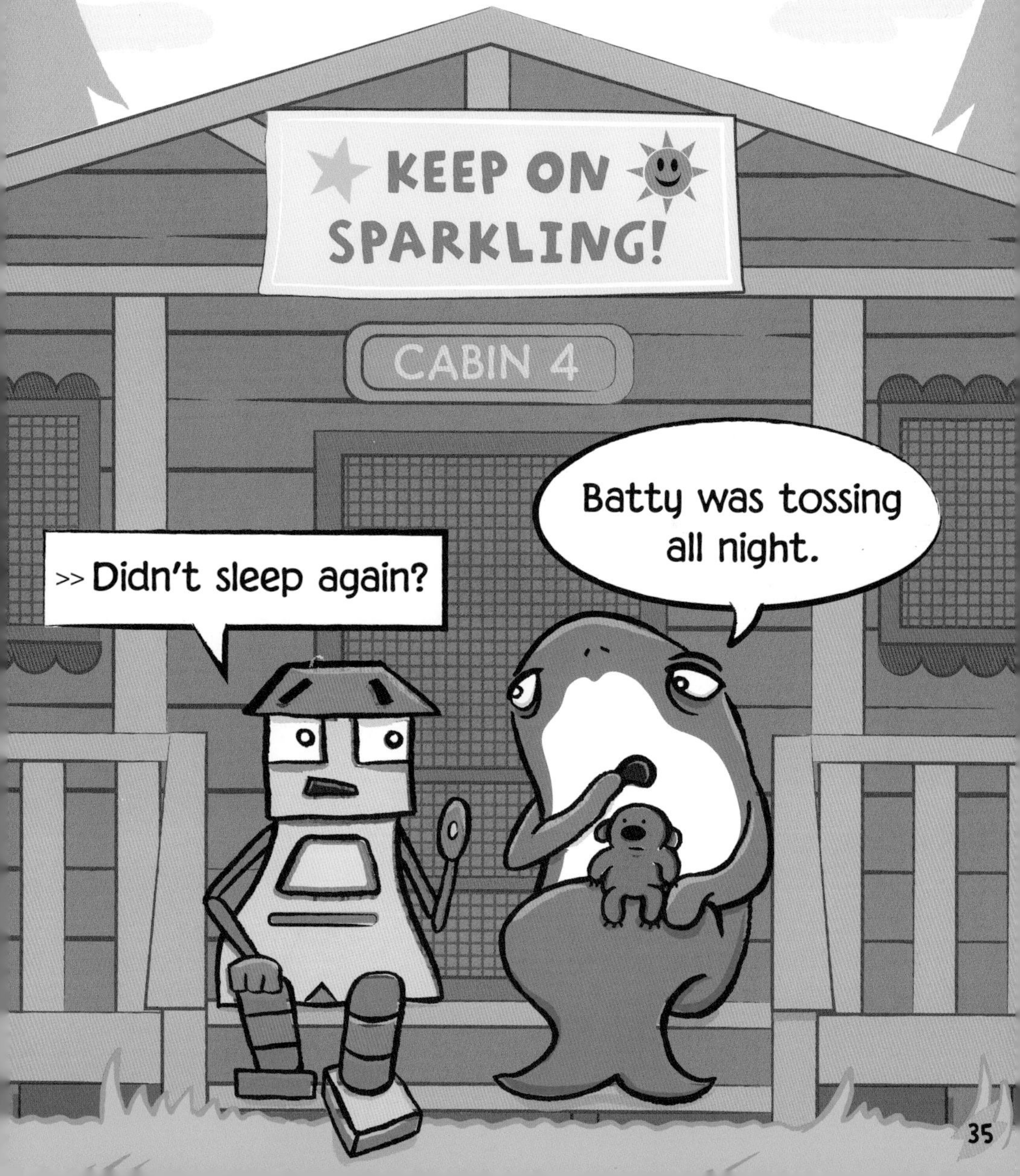
KEEP ON SPARKLING!
CABIN 4
>> Didn't sleep again?
Batty was tossing all night.

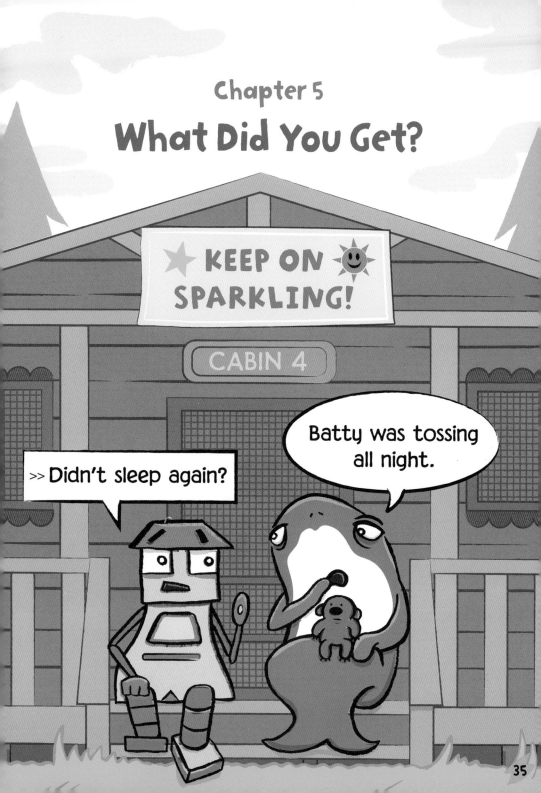

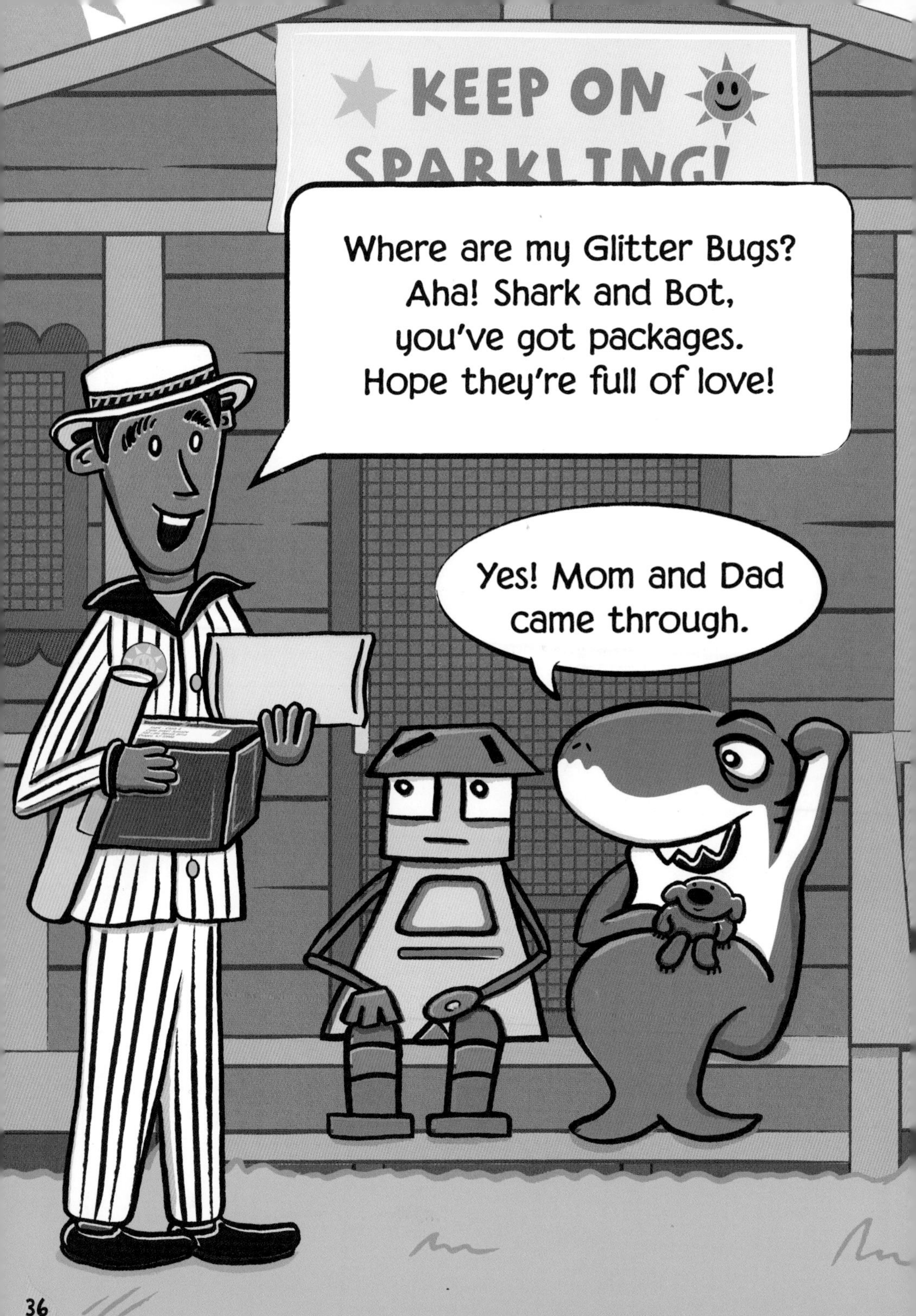
KEEP ON SPARKLING!
Where are my Glitter Bugs? Aha! Shark and Bot, you've got packages. Hope they're full of love!
Yes! Mom and Dad came through.

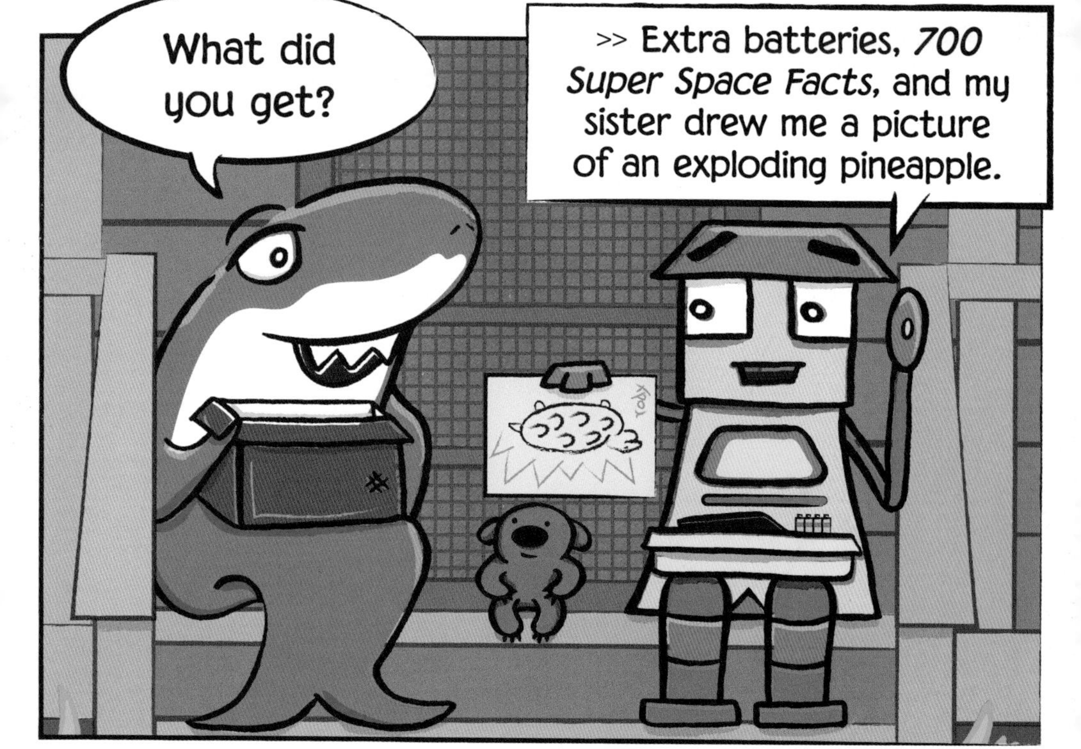
What did you get?
>> Extra batteries, *700 Super Space Facts*, and my sister drew me a picture of an exploding pineapple.
Tody

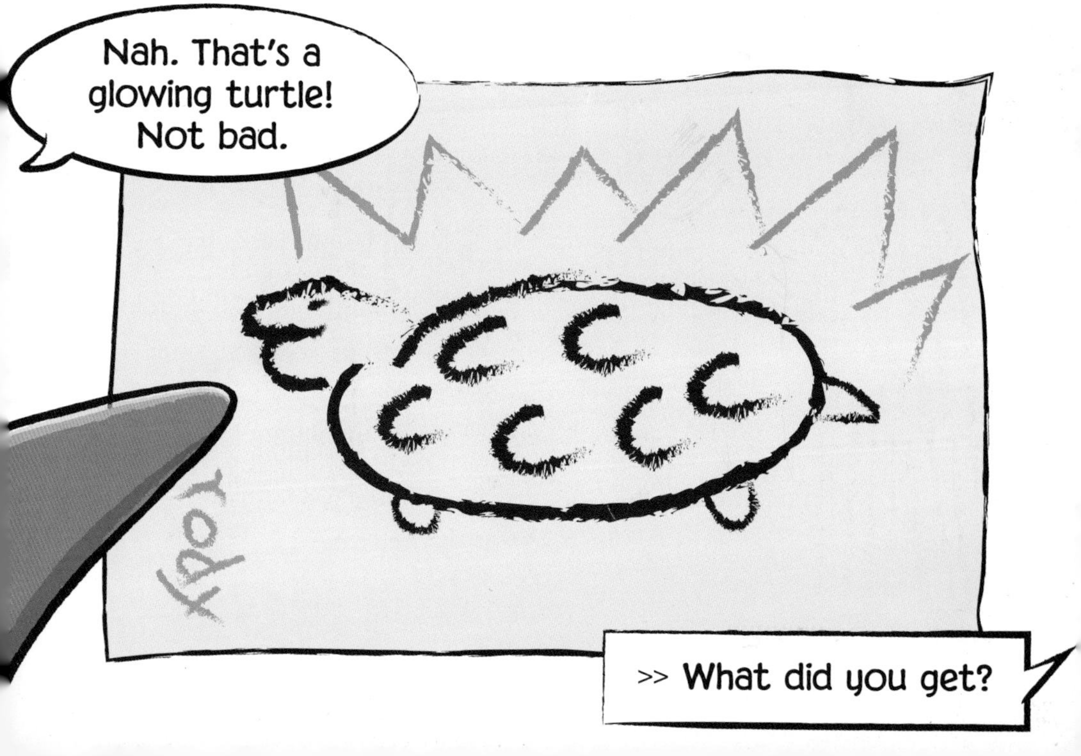
Nah. That's a glowing turtle! Not bad.
Tody
>> What did you get?

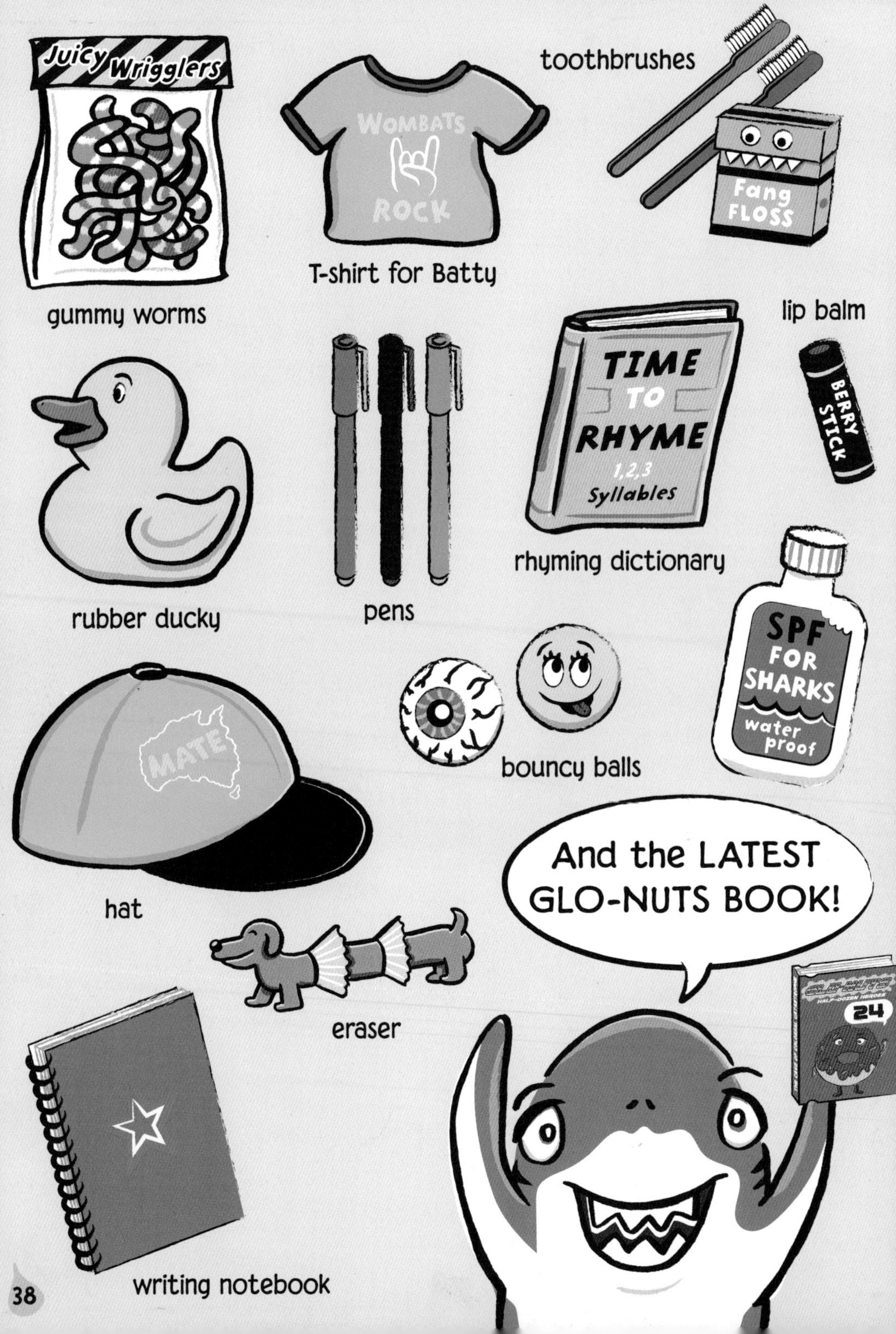
Juicy Wrigglers
gummy worms
WOMBATS ROCK
T-shirt for Batty
toothbrushes
Fang FLOSS
lip balm
BERRY STICK
TIME TO RHYME
1,2,3
Syllables
rhyming dictionary
rubber ducky
pens
SPF FOR SHARKS
water proof
bouncy balls
MATE
hat
eraser
And the LATEST GLO-NUTS BOOK!
24
writing notebook

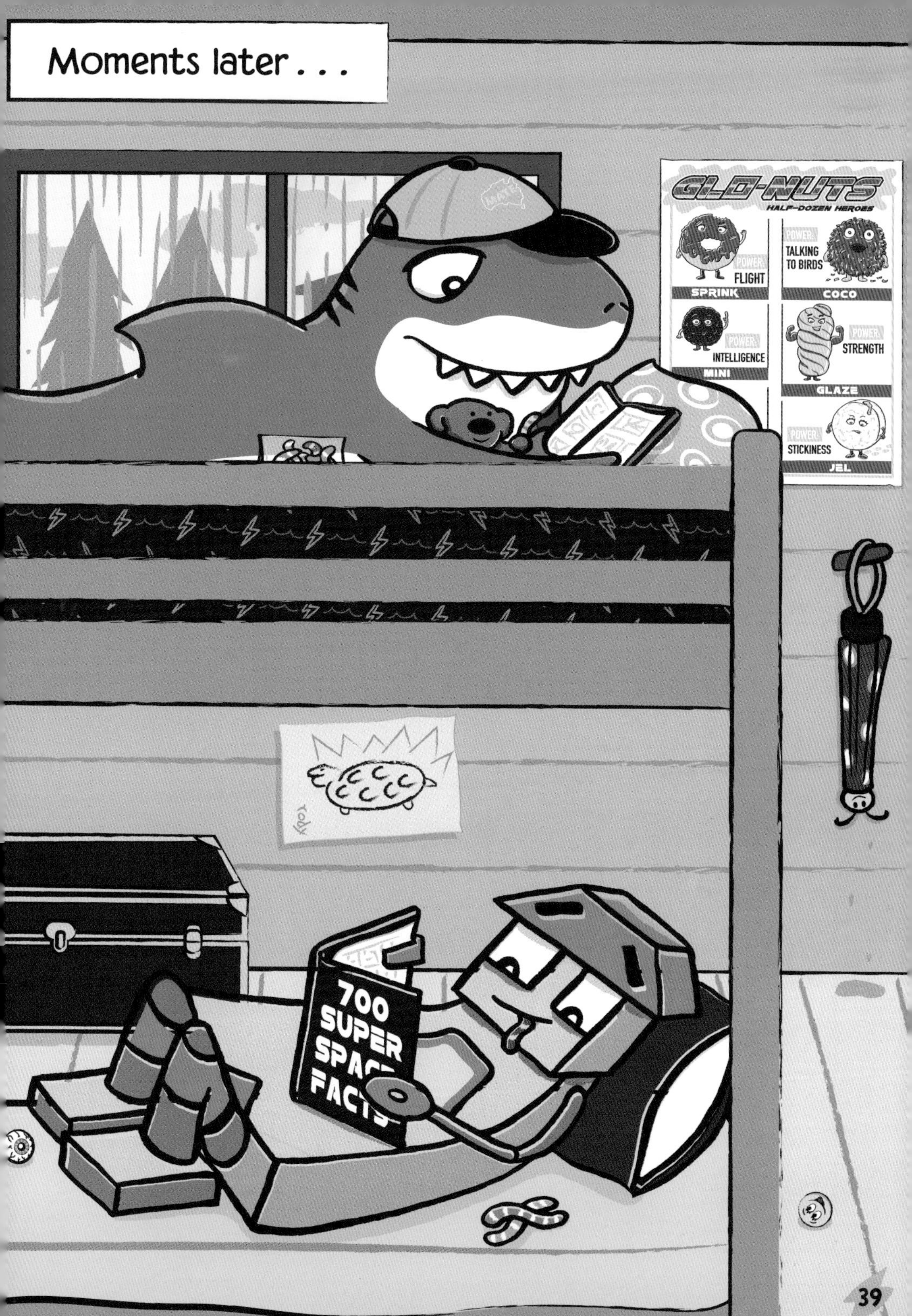
Moments later . . .
MATE
GLO-NUTS
HALF-DOZEN HEROES
POWER: FLIGHT
SPRINK
POWER: TALKING TO BIRDS
COCO
POWER: INTELLIGENCE
MINI
POWER: STRENGTH
GLAZE
POWER: STICKINESS
JEL
Toby
700 SUPER SPAC FACTS

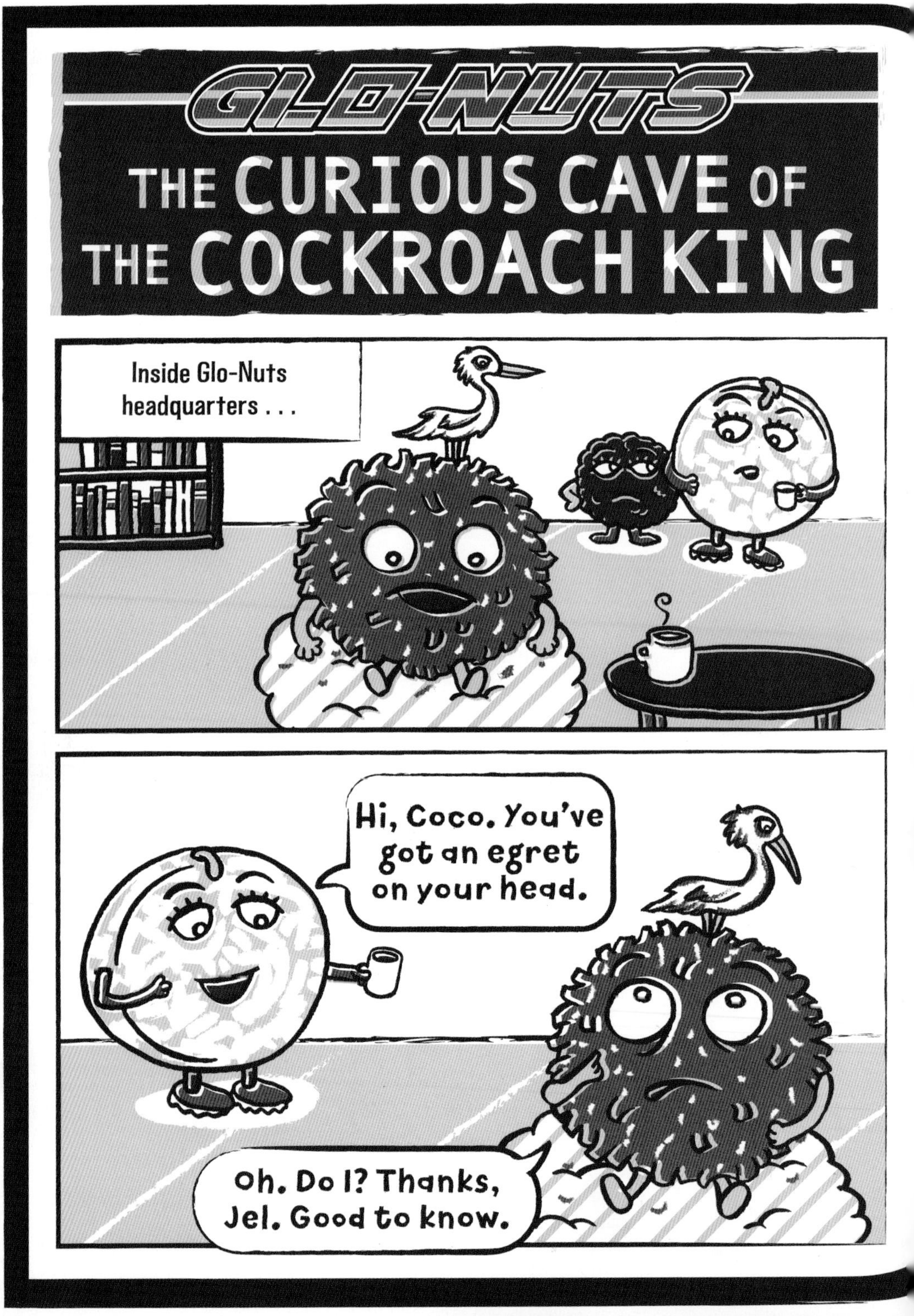
GLO-NUTS
THE CURIOUS CAVE OF THE COCKROACH KING
Inside Glo-Nuts headquarters . . .
Hi, Coco. You've got an egret on your head.
Oh. Do I? Thanks, Jel. Good to know.

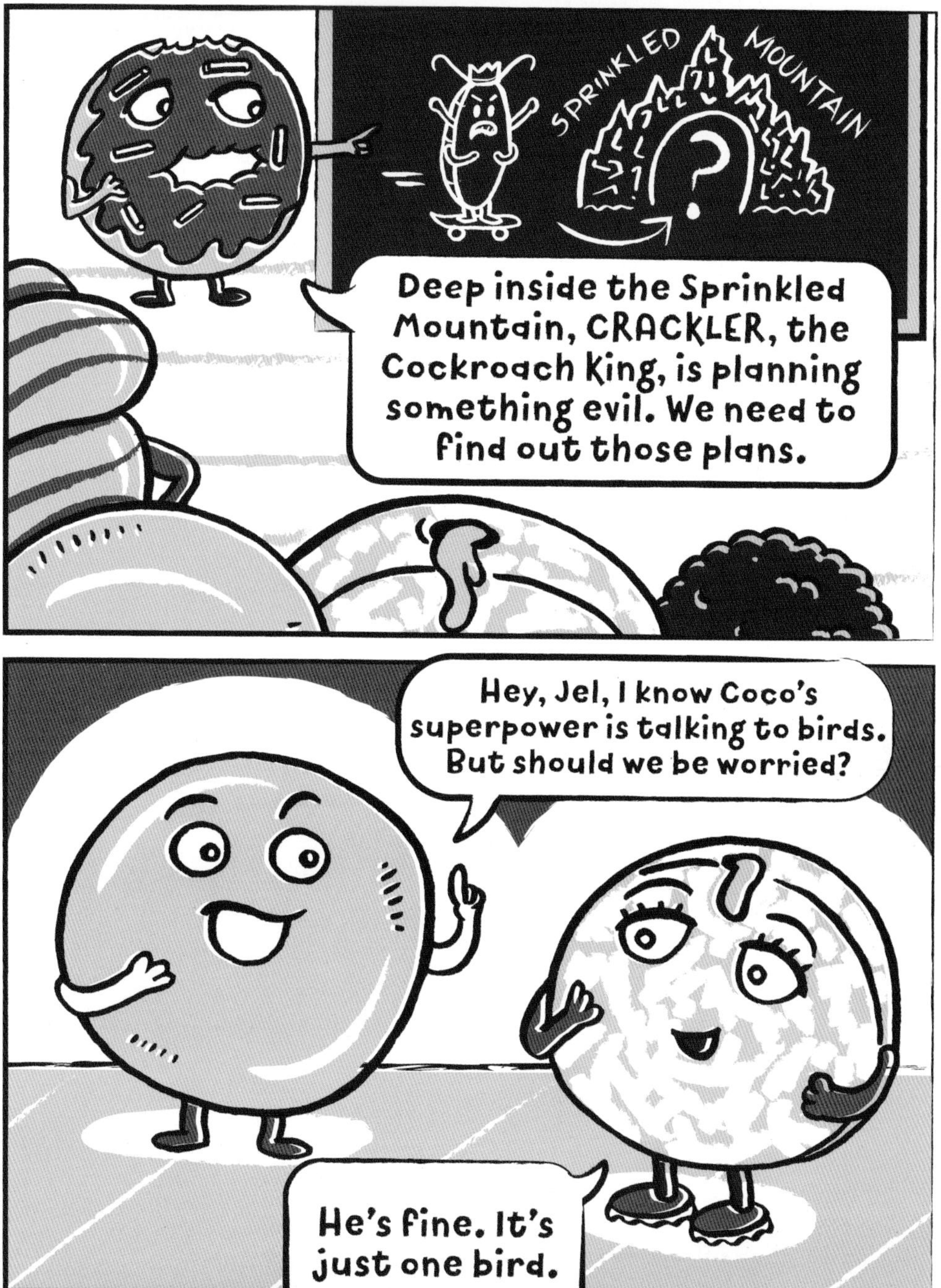
SPRINKLED MOUNTAIN
Deep inside the Sprinkled Mountain, CRACKLER, the Cockroach King, is planning something evil. We need to find out those plans.
Hey, Jel, I know Coco's superpower is talking to birds. But should we be worried?
He's fine. It's just one bird.

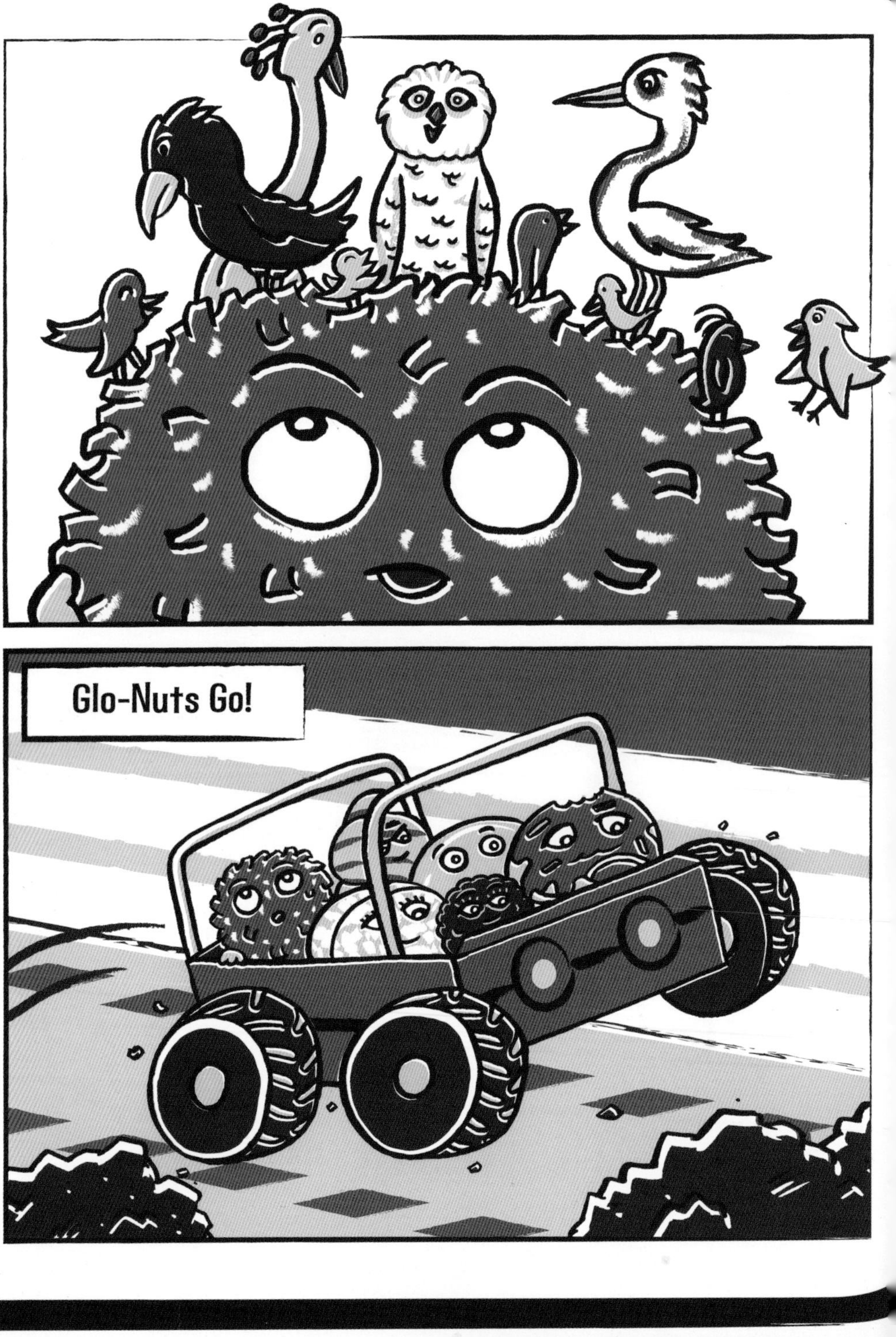
Glo-Nuts Go!

Chapter 6

Talent Takes Practice

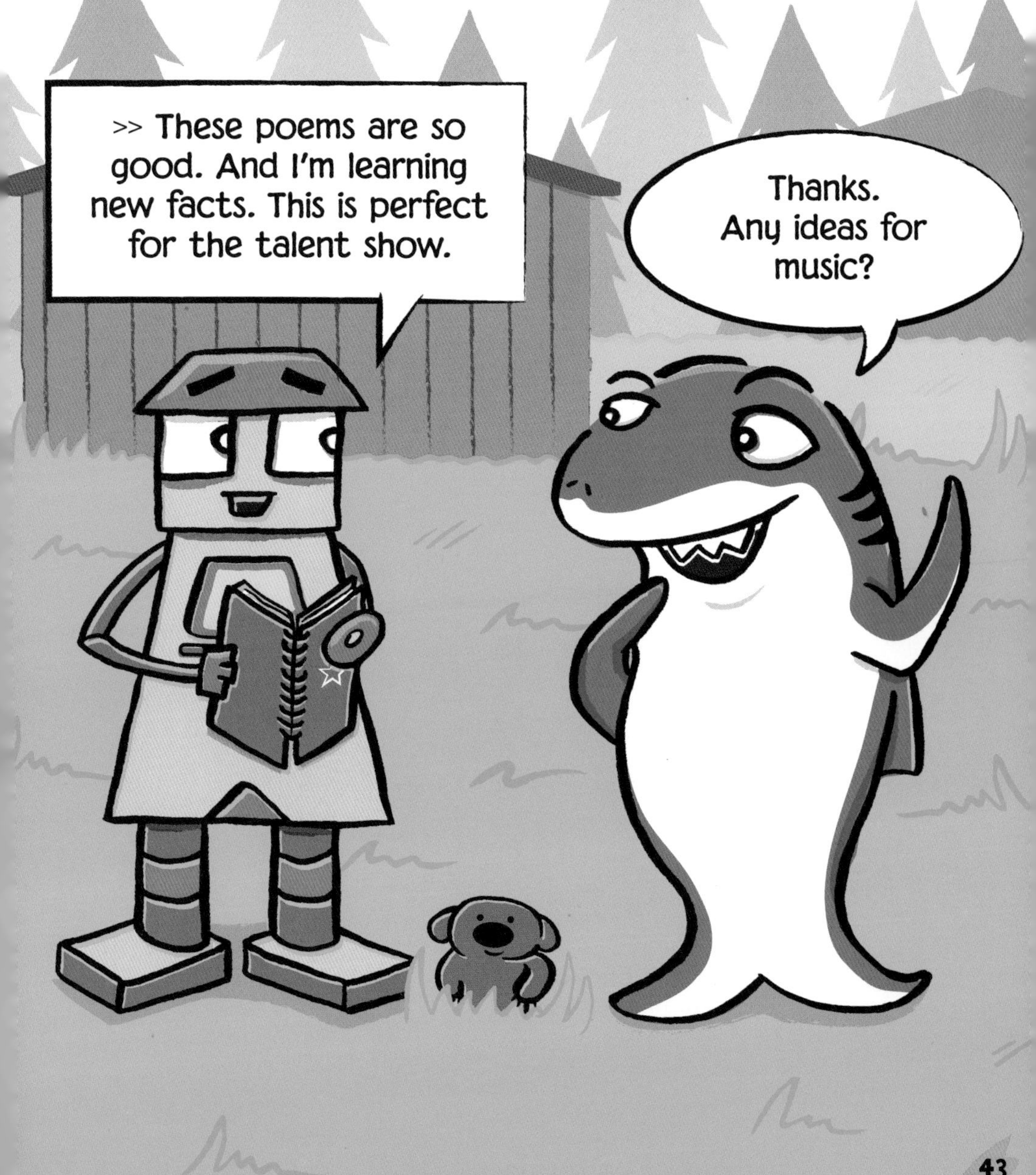
>> These poems are so good. And I'm learning new facts. This is perfect for the talent show.
Thanks. Any ideas for music?

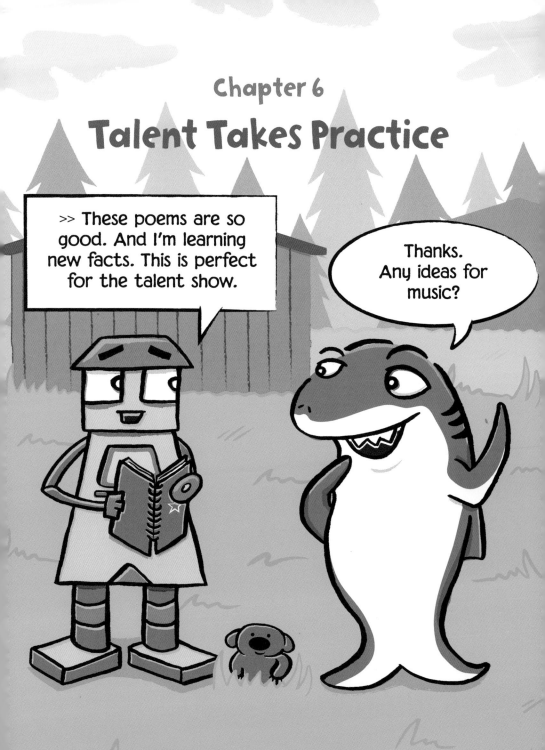

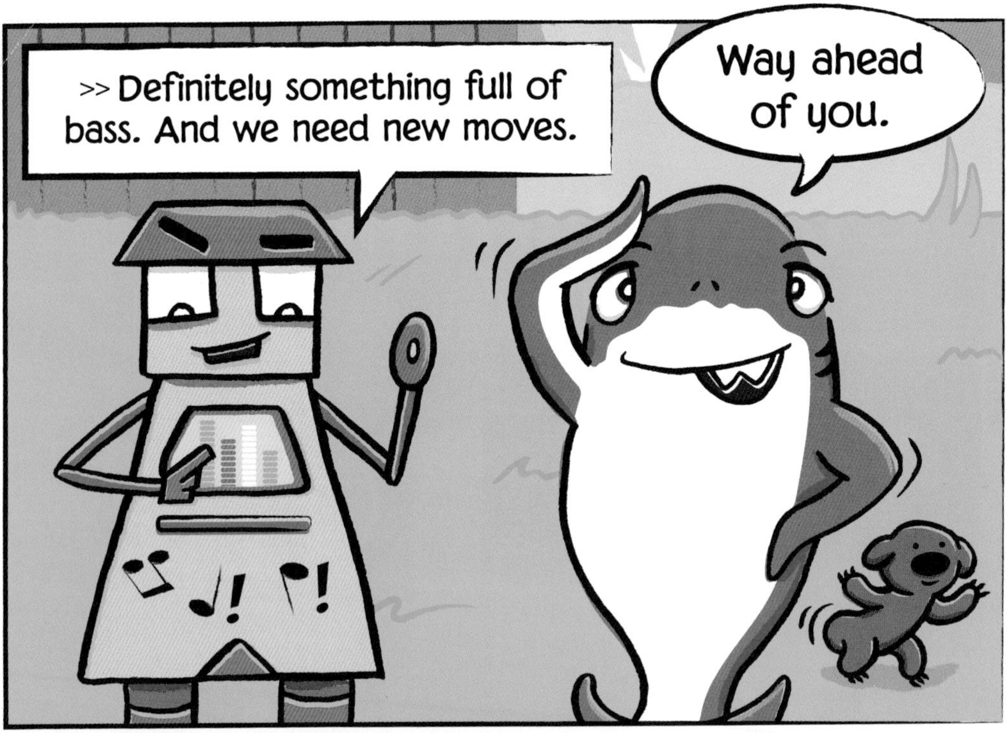
>> Definitely something full of bass. And we need new moves.
Way ahead of you.

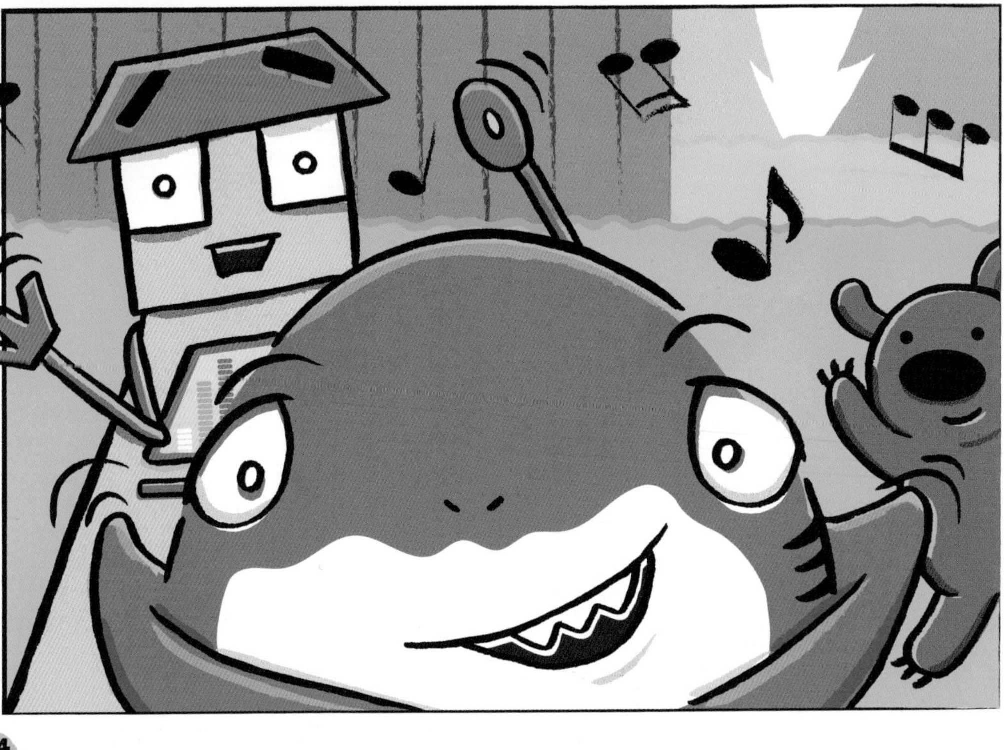

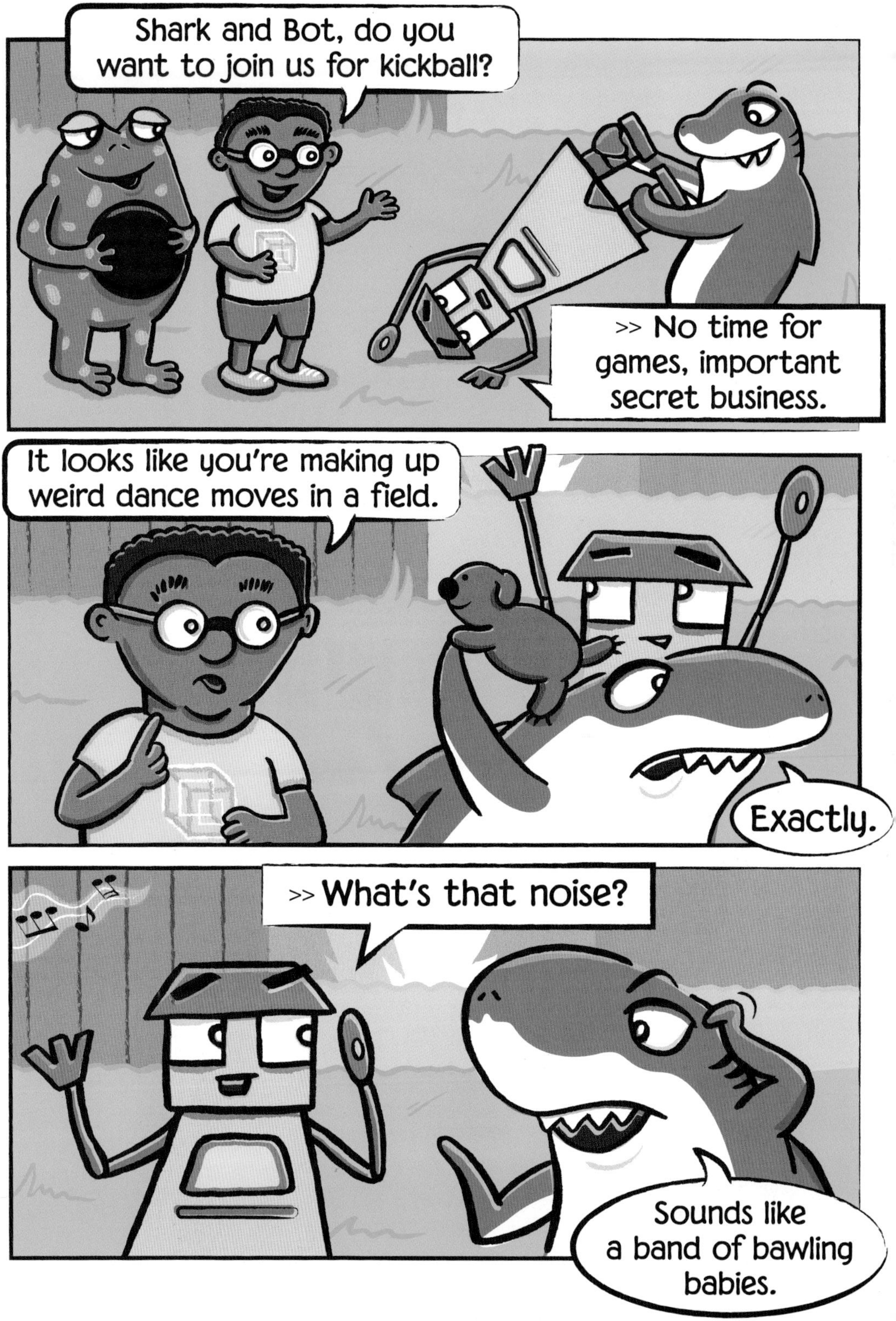
Shark and Bot, do you want to join us for kickball?
>> No time for games, important secret business.
It looks like you're making up weird dance moves in a field.
Exactly.
>> What's that noise?
Sounds like a band of bawling babies.

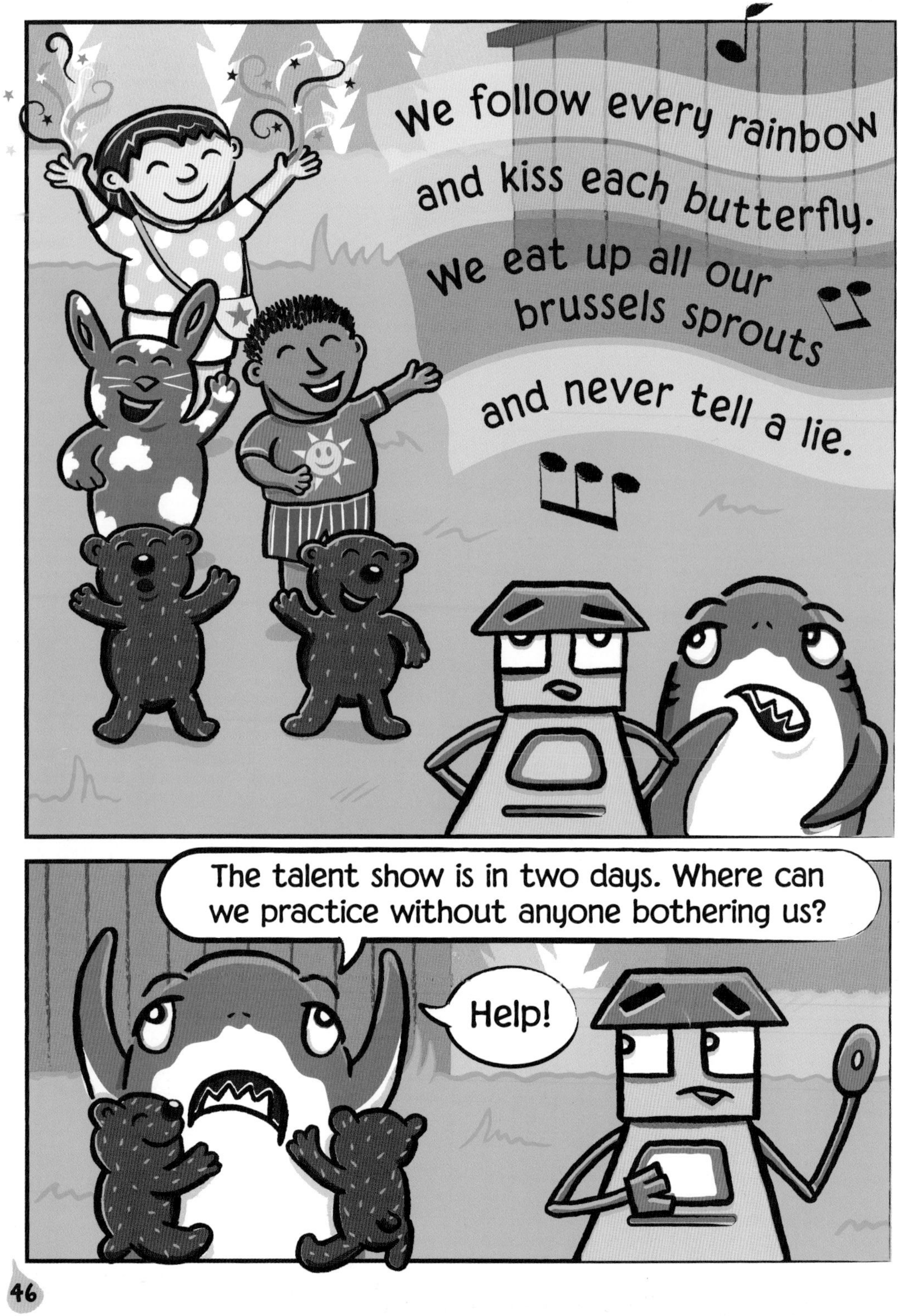
We follow every rainbow
and kiss each butterfly.
We eat up all our
brussels sprouts
and never tell a lie.
The talent show is in two days. Where can we practice without anyone bothering us?
Help!

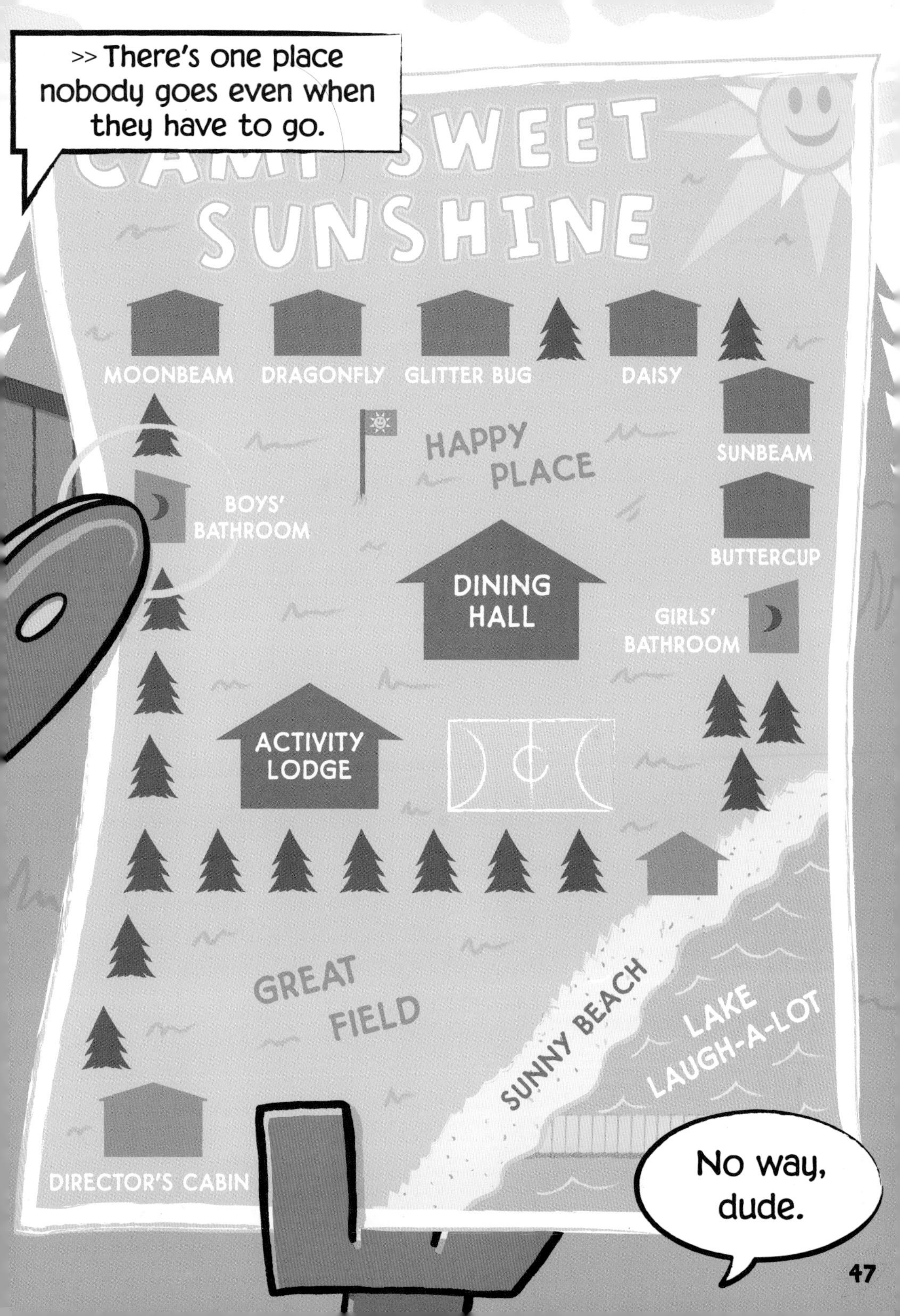

>> There's one place nobody goes even when they have to go.
CAMP SWEET SUNSHINE
MOONBEAM
DRAGONFLY
GLITTER BUG
DAISY
SUNBEAM
HAPPY PLACE
BOYS' BATHROOM
BUTTERCUP
DINING HALL
GIRLS' BATHROOM
ACTIVITY LODGE
GREAT FIELD
SUNNY BEACH
LAKE LAUGH-A-LOT
DIRECTOR'S CABIN
No way, dude.

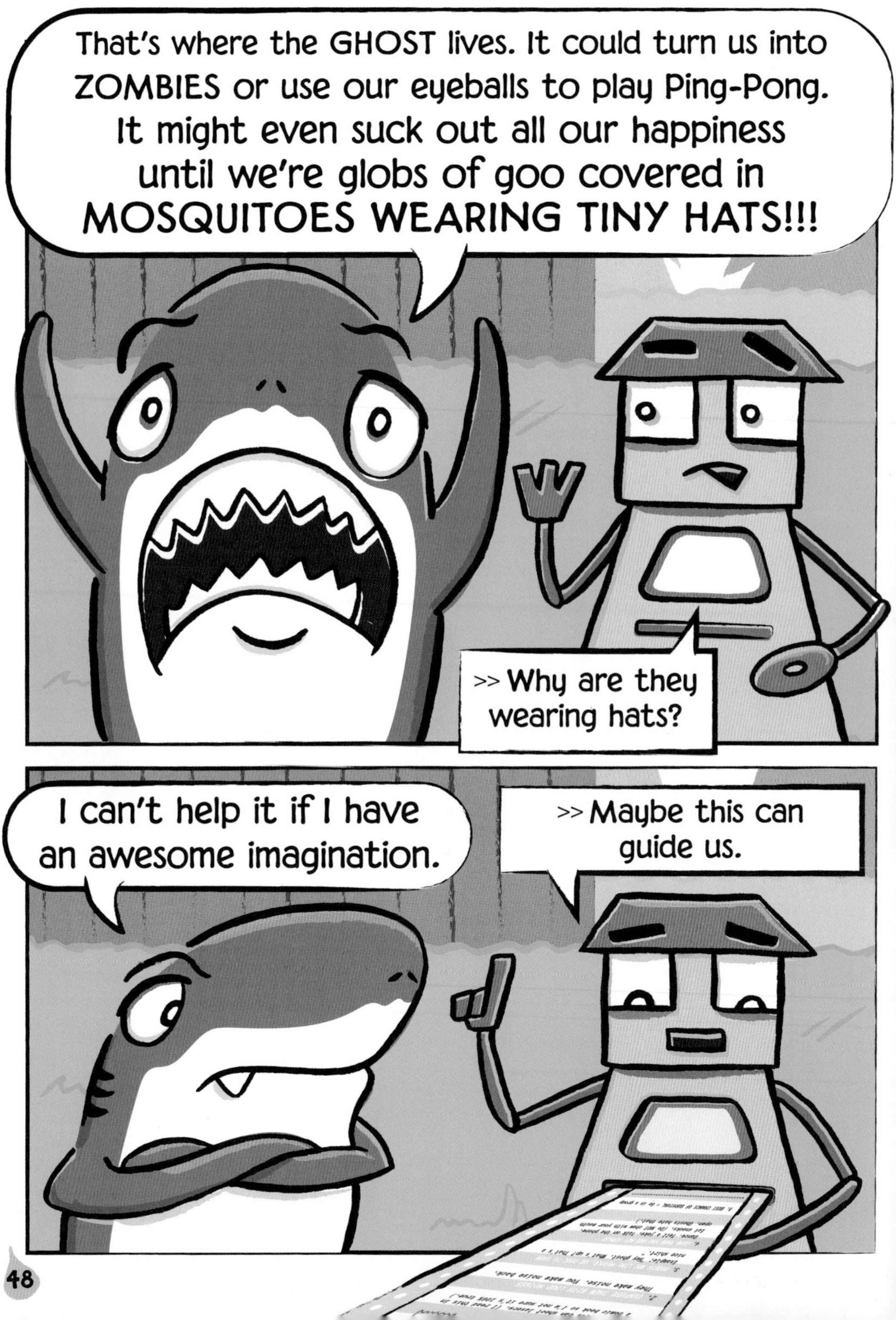
That's where the GHOST lives. It could turn us into ZOMBIES or use our eyeballs to play Ping-Pong. It might even suck out all our happiness until we're globs of goo covered in MOSQUITOES WEARING TINY HATS!!!
>> Why are they wearing hats?
I can't help it if I have an awesome imagination.
>> Maybe this can guide us.

HOW TO SURVIVE A
GHOST MEETING

by Bot

 <--- very scary ghost

****

1. WEAR PROTECTION.

Some ghosts can shoot lasers. (I read this in
a comic book so I'm not sure it's 100% true.)

2. CONFUSE THEM WITH LOUD NOISES.

They make noise; you make noise back.

3. GHOSTS ARE LIKE EVERYONE ELSE.

Be cool to them. Example: "Hey, ghost. What's up?
That's a nice shirt."

4. SHOW THEM YOU ARE NOT AFRAID.

Dance. Tell a joke. Eat snacks.
(Do NOT chew with your mouth open. Ghosts hate that.)

5. BEST CHANCE OF SURVIVAL = go in a group

****

Chapter 7
Ghost Hunting

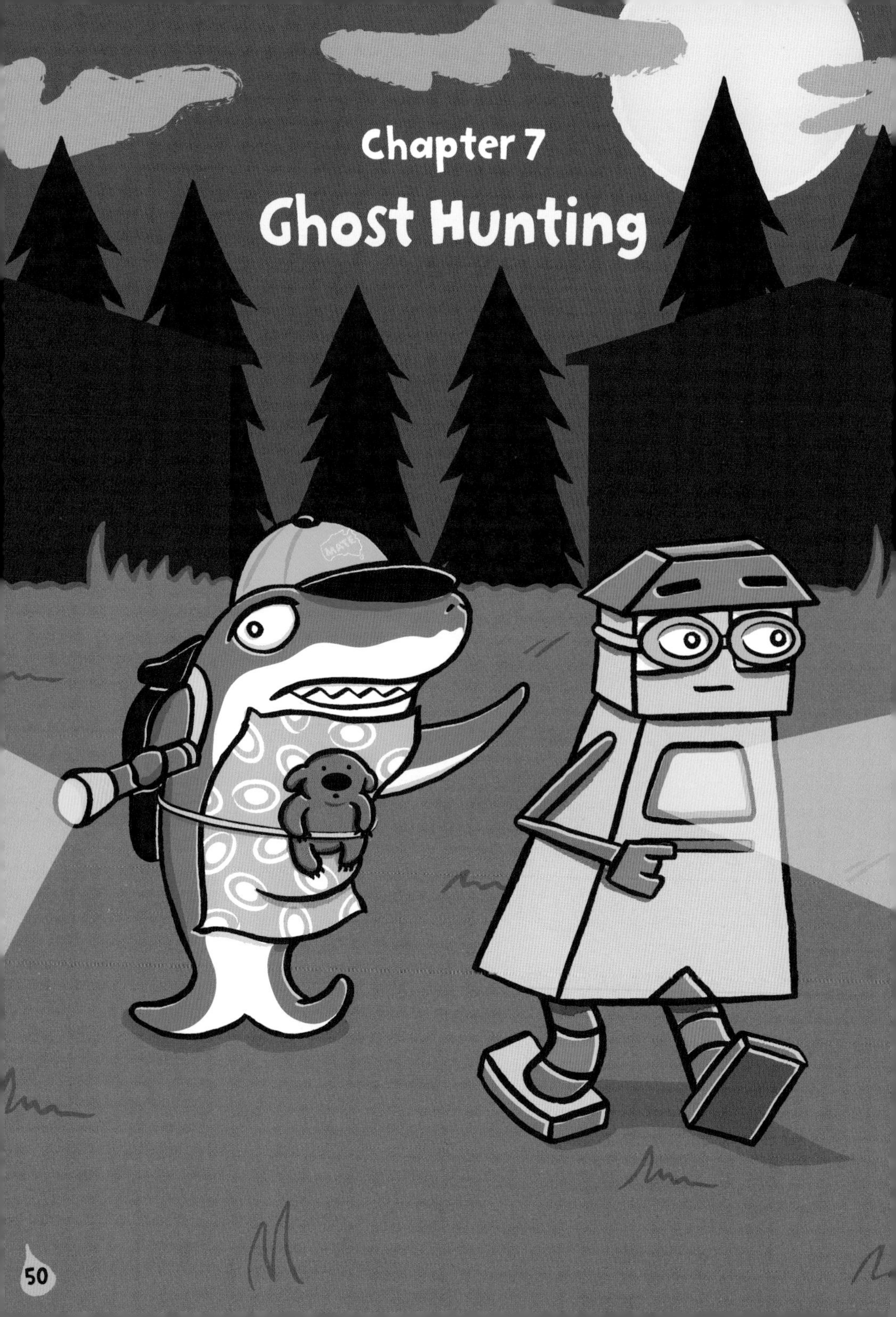
MATE

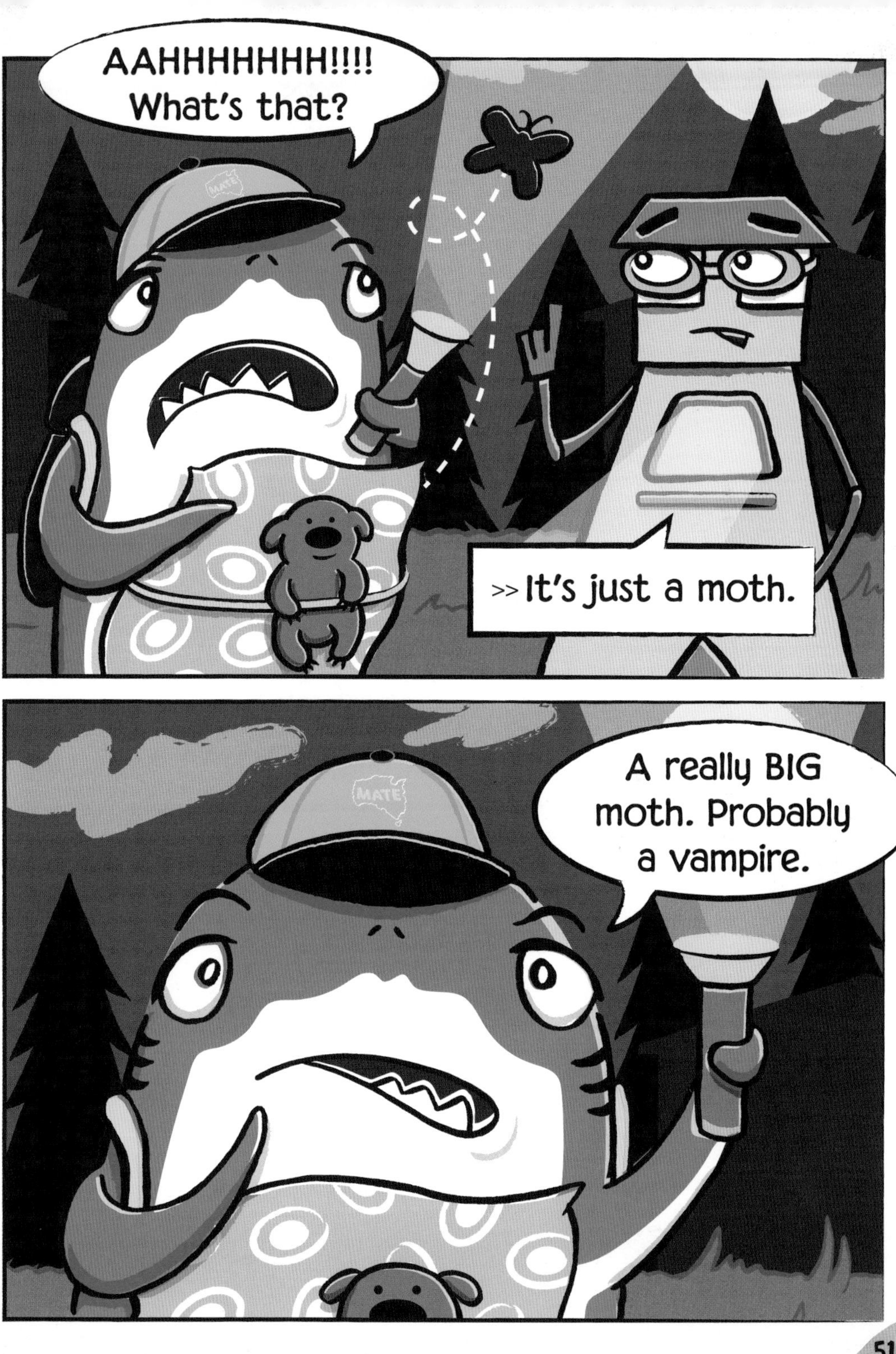
AAHHHHHHH!!!!! What's that?
>> It's just a moth.
A really BIG moth. Probably a vampire.

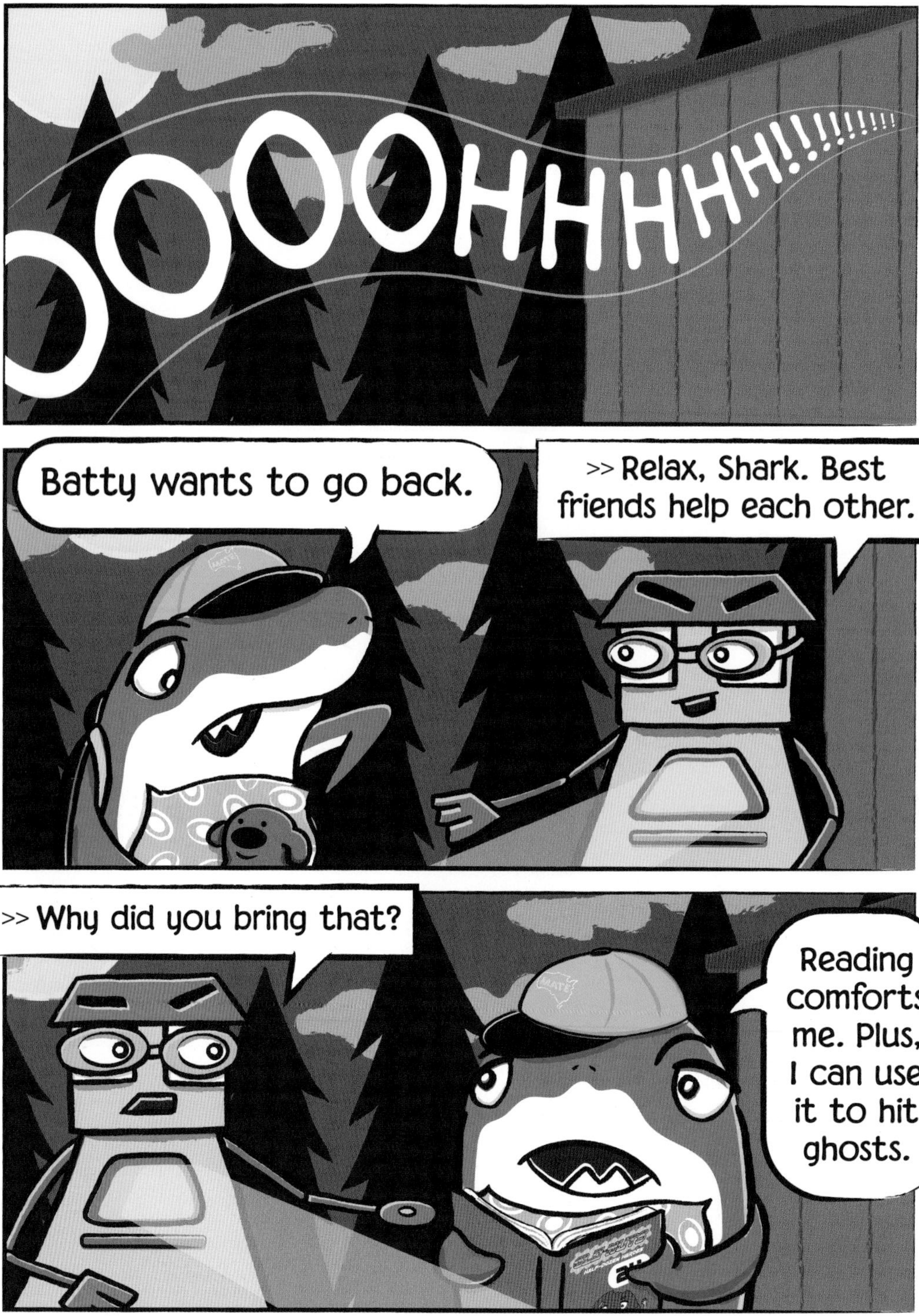
OOOOOHHHHHH!!!!!!!!!
Batty wants to go back.
>> Relax, Shark. Best friends help each other.
>> Why did you bring that?
Reading comforts me. Plus, I can use it to hit ghosts.

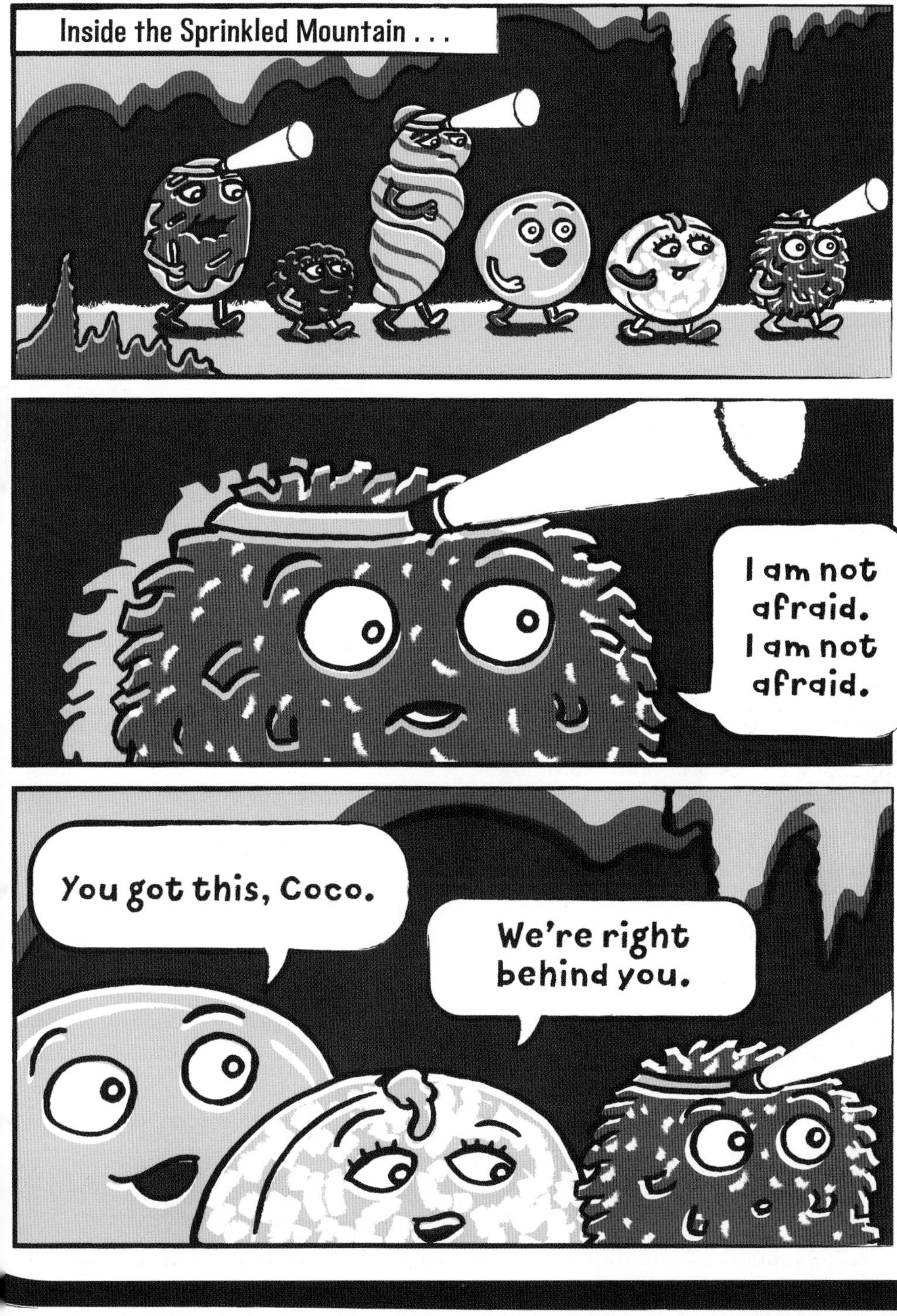

Inside the Sprinkled Mountain . . .
I am not afraid. I am not afraid.
You got this, Coco.
We're right behind you.

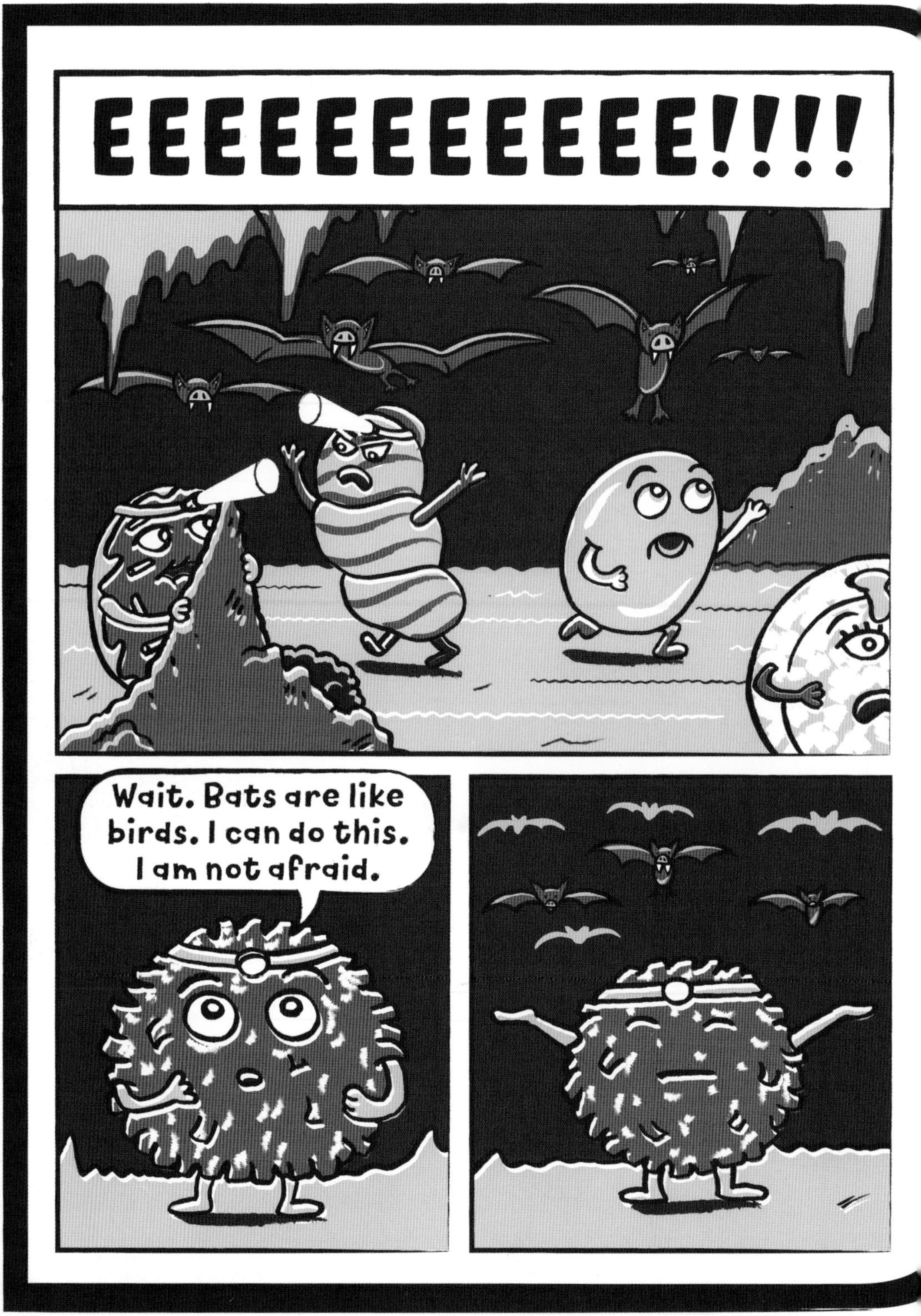
EEEEEEEEEEEEE!!!!
Wait. Bats are like birds. I can do this. I am not afraid.

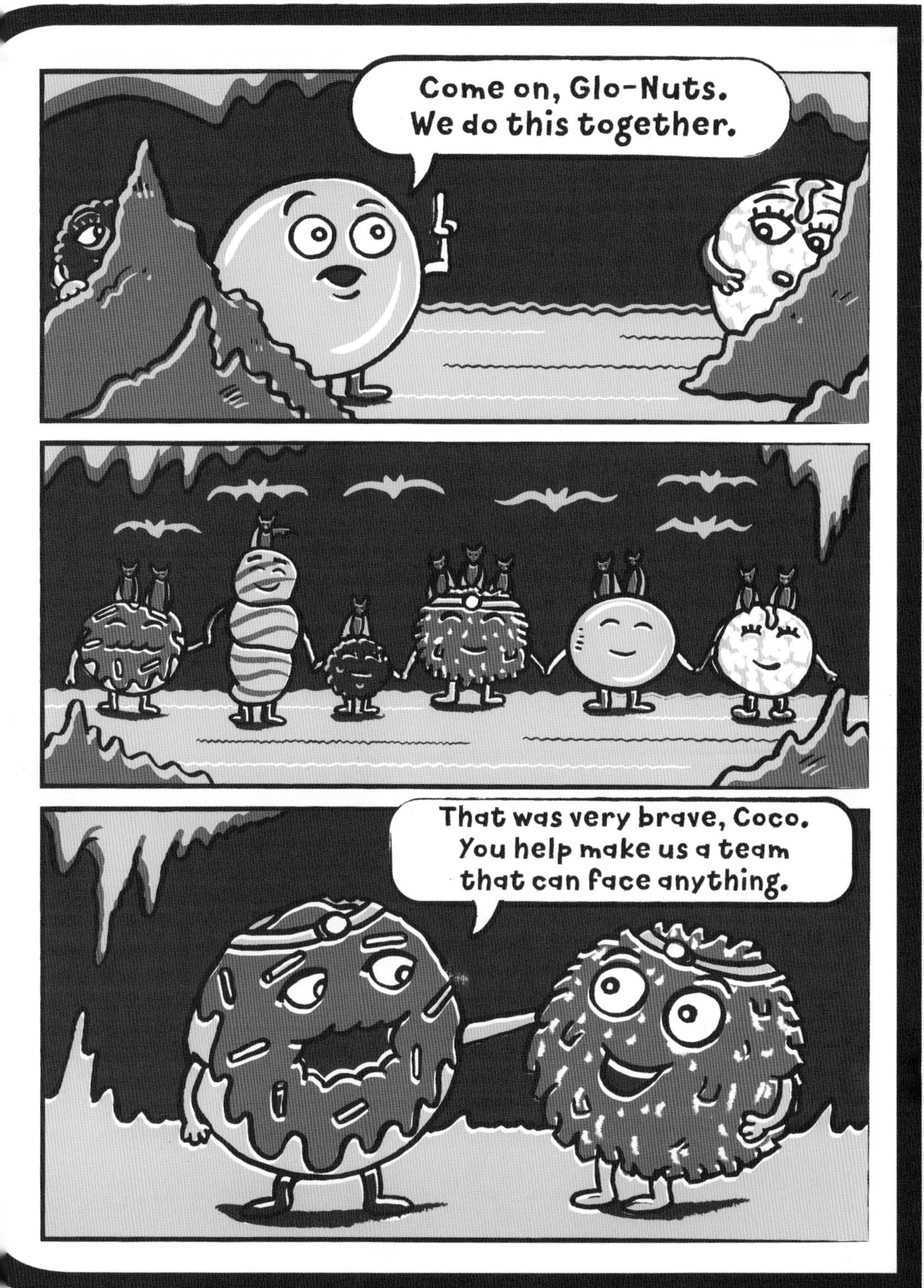
Come on, Glo-Nuts. We do this together.
That was very brave, Coco. You help make us a team that can face anything.

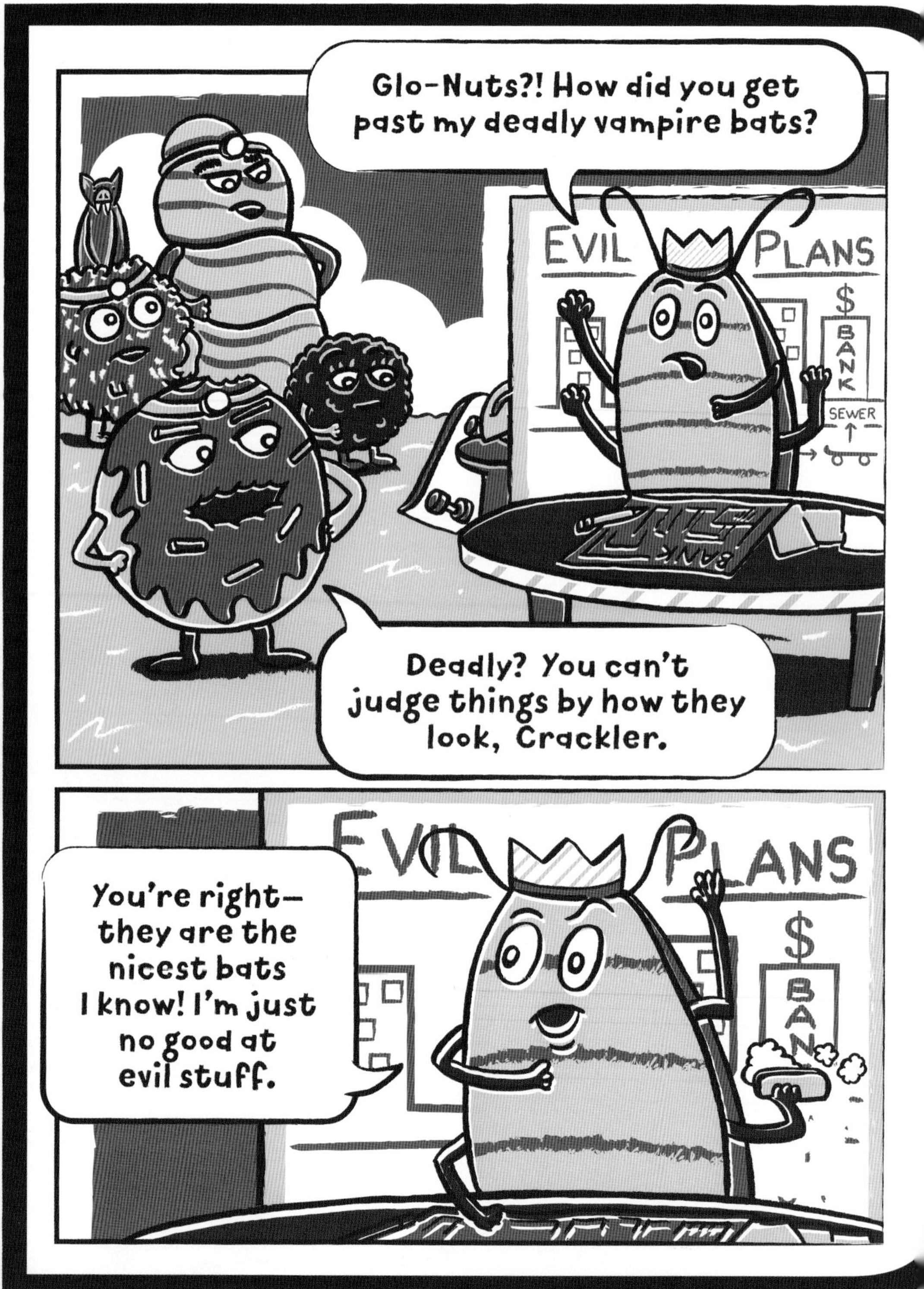
Glo-Nuts?! How did you get past my deadly vampire bats?
EVIL PLANS
BANK
SEWER
Deadly? You can't judge things by how they look, Crackler.
EVIL PLANS
You're right—they are the nicest bats I know! I'm just no good at evil stuff.

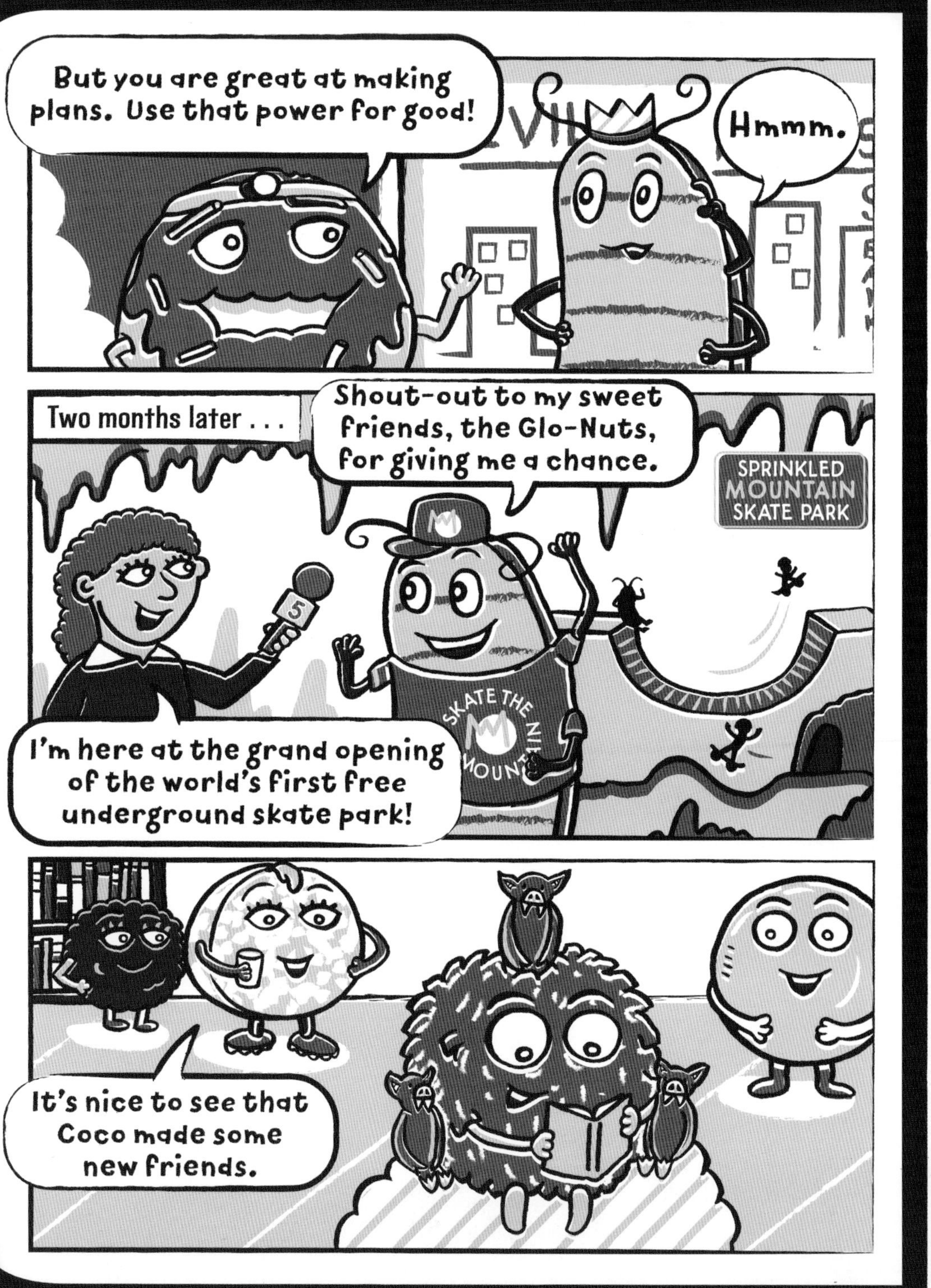

But you are great at making plans. Use that power for good!
Hmmm.
Two months later . . .
Shout-out to my sweet friends, the Glo-Nuts, for giving me a chance.
SPRINKLED MOUNTAIN SKATE PARK
I'm here at the grand opening of the world's first free underground skate park!
It's nice to see that Coco made some new friends.

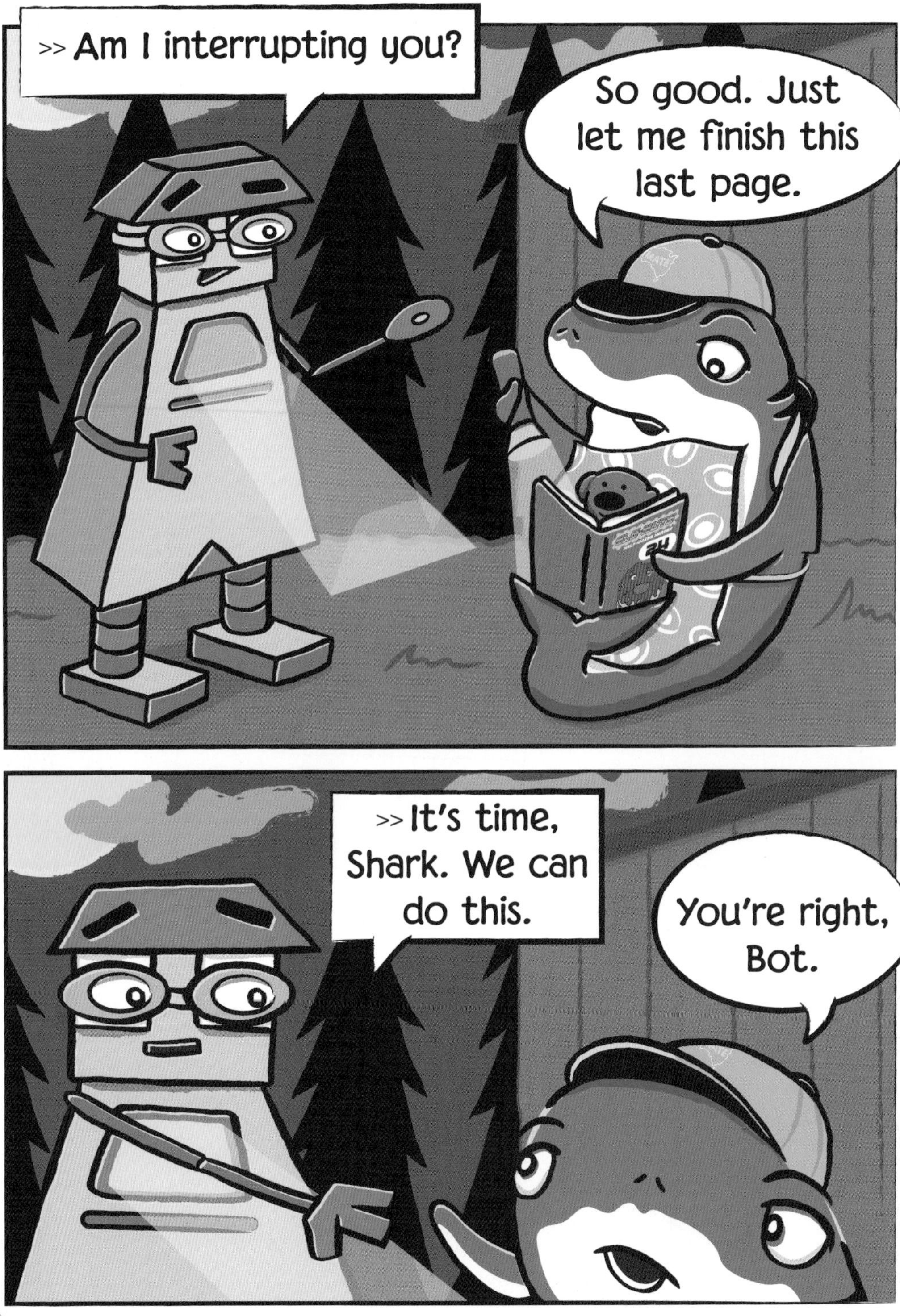
>> Am I interrupting you?
So good. Just let me finish this last page.
>> It's time, Shark. We can do this.
You're right, Bot.

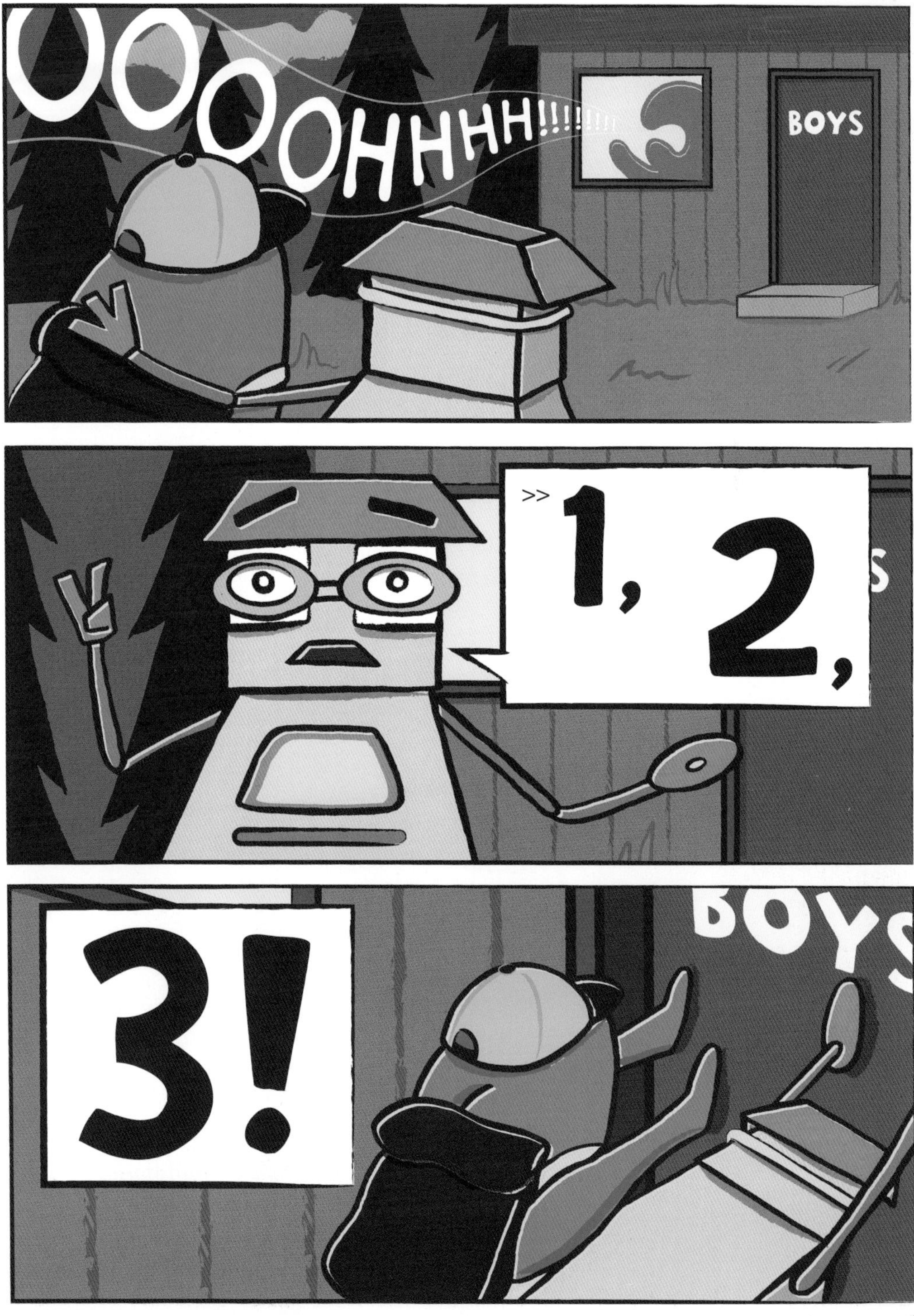
OOOOOHHHHH!!!!!!!!
BOYS
>> 1, 2,
3!
BOYS

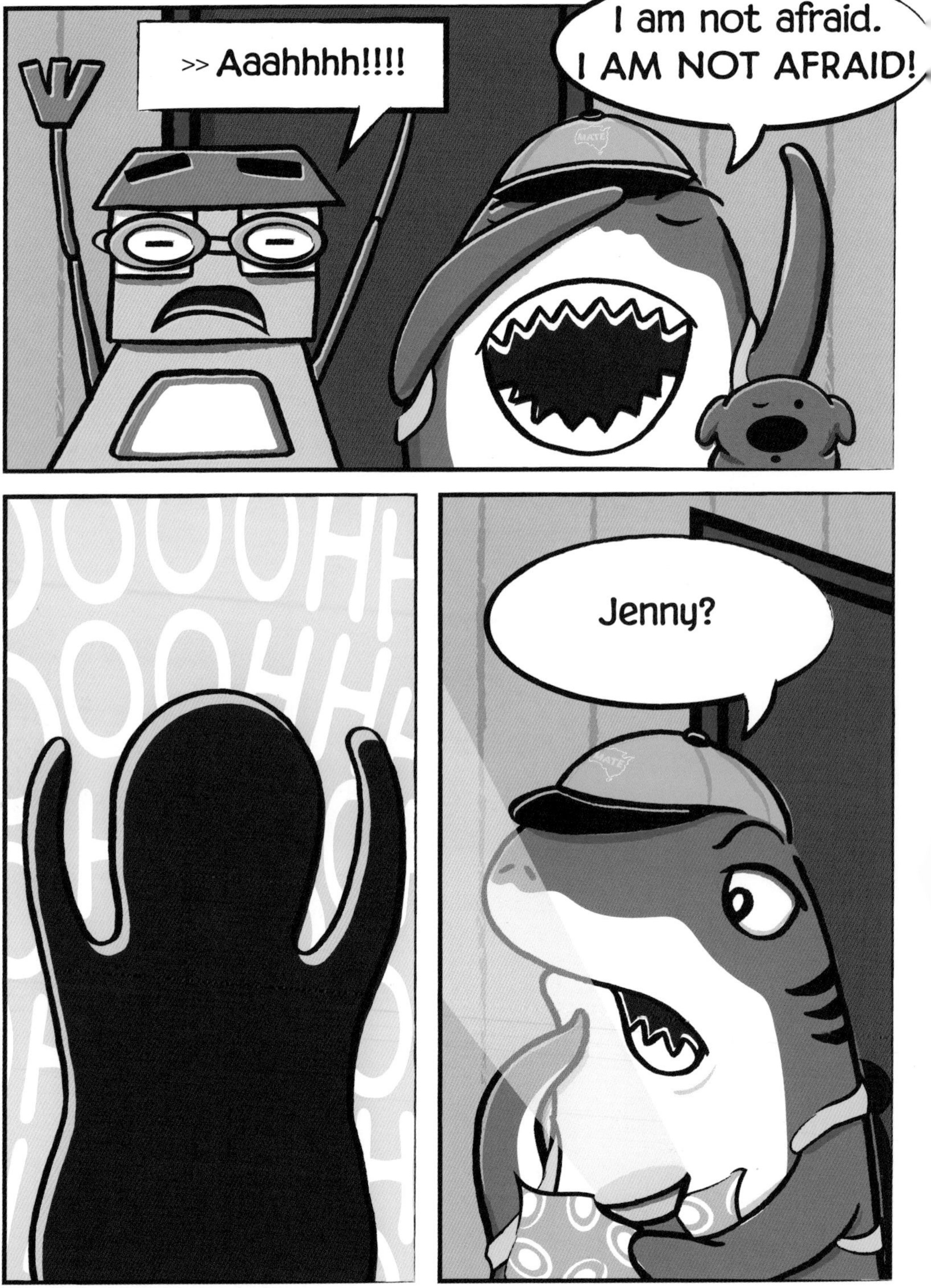
>> Aaahhhh!!!!
I am not afraid.
I AM NOT AFRAID!
MATE
Jenny?
MATE

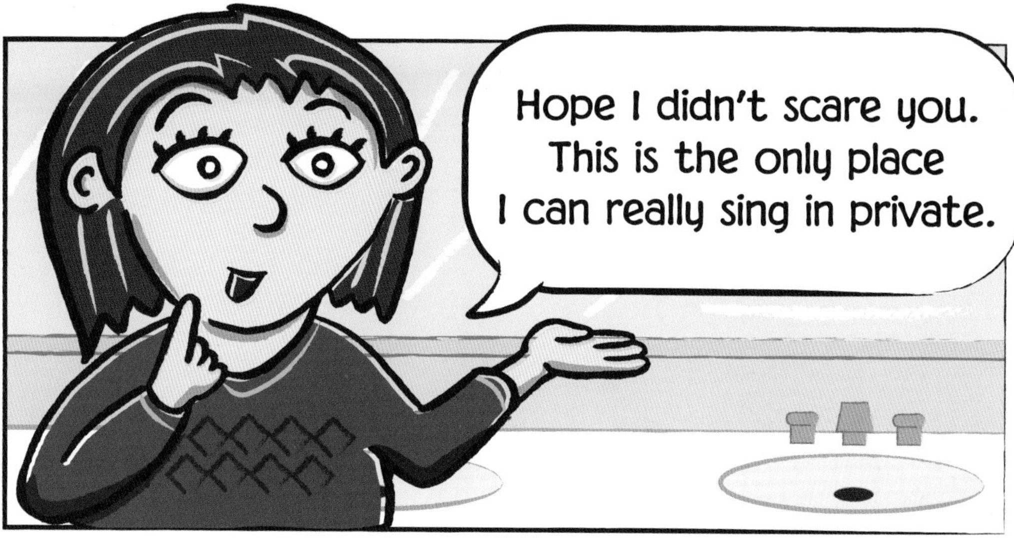
Hope I didn't scare you. This is the only place I can really sing in private.

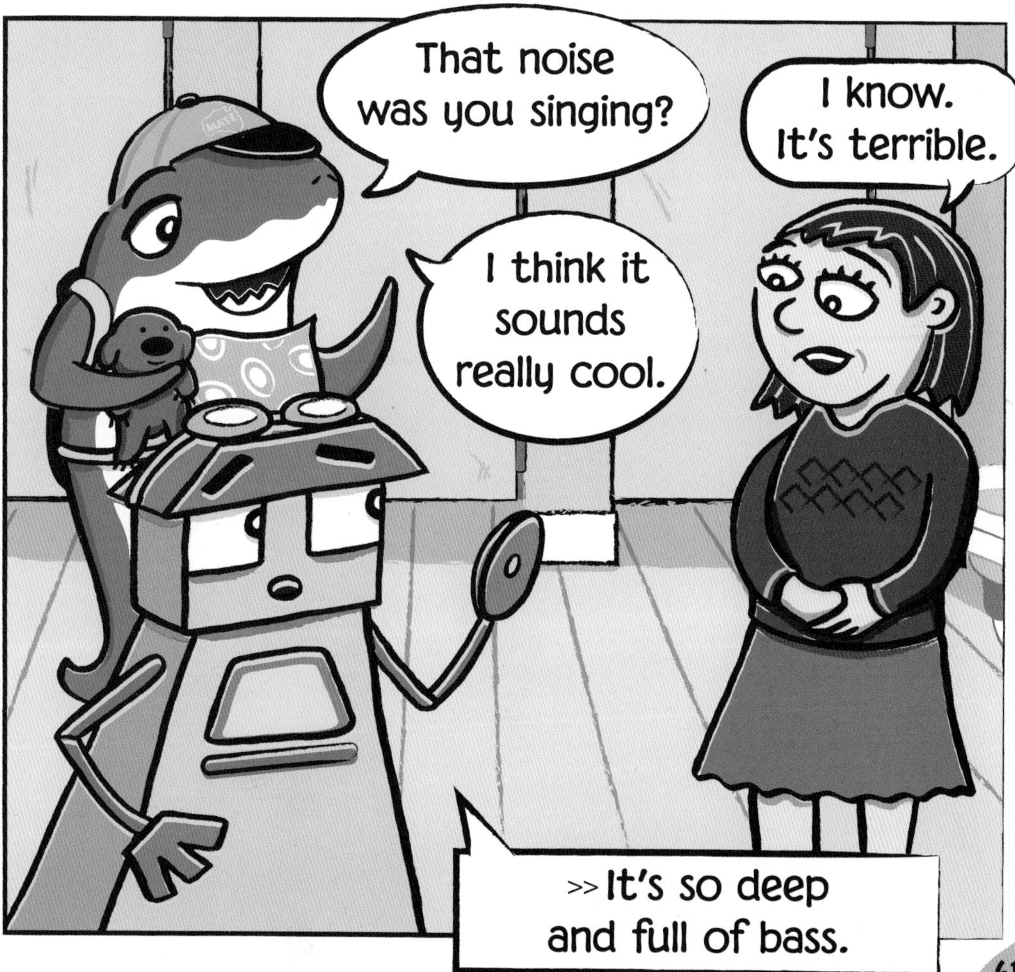
That noise was you singing?
I know. It's terrible.
I think it sounds really cool.
>> It's so deep and full of bass.

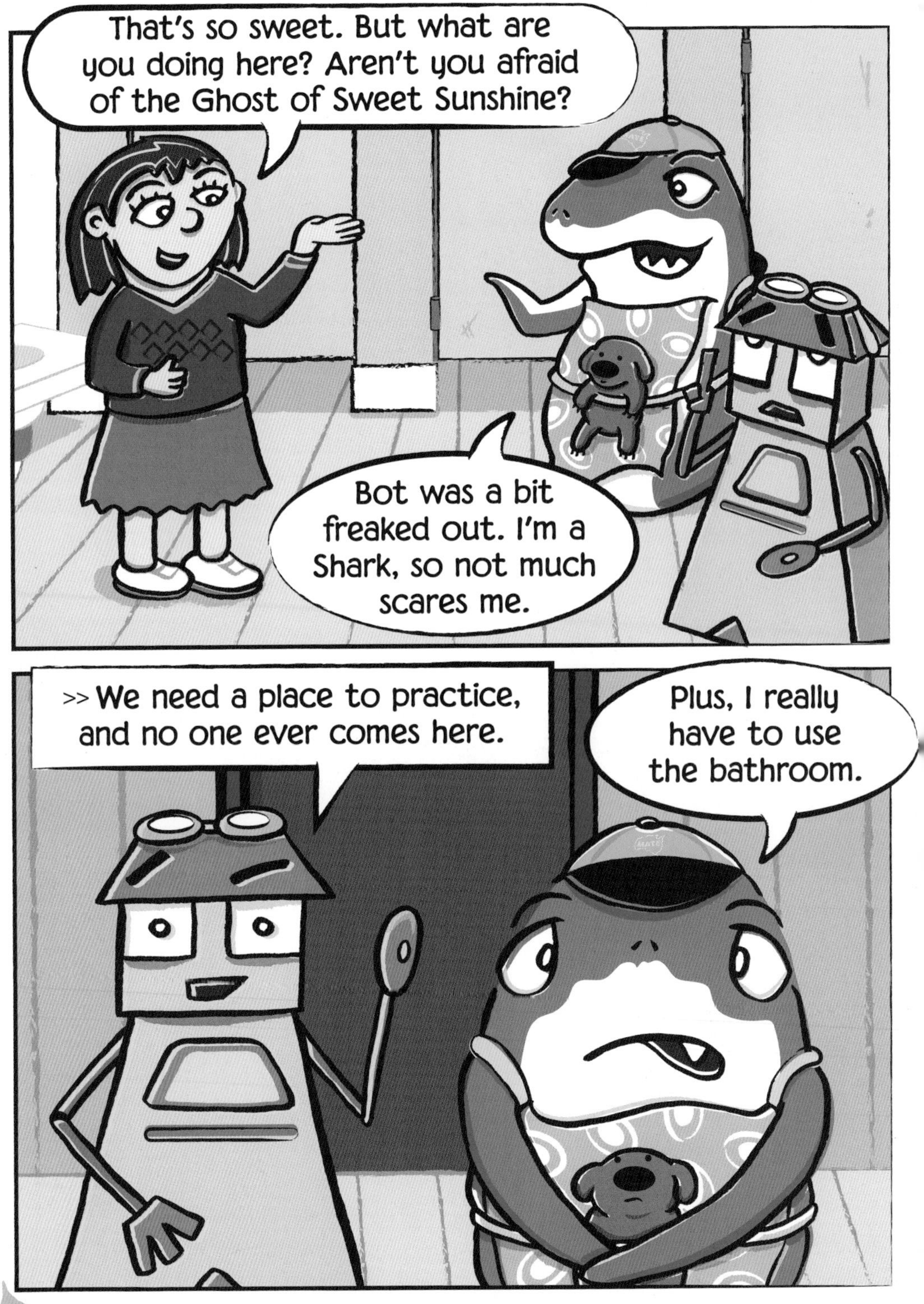
That's so sweet. But what are you doing here? Aren't you afraid of the Ghost of Sweet Sunshine?
Bot was a bit freaked out. I'm a Shark, so not much scares me.
>> We need a place to practice, and no one ever comes here.
Plus, I really have to use the bathroom.

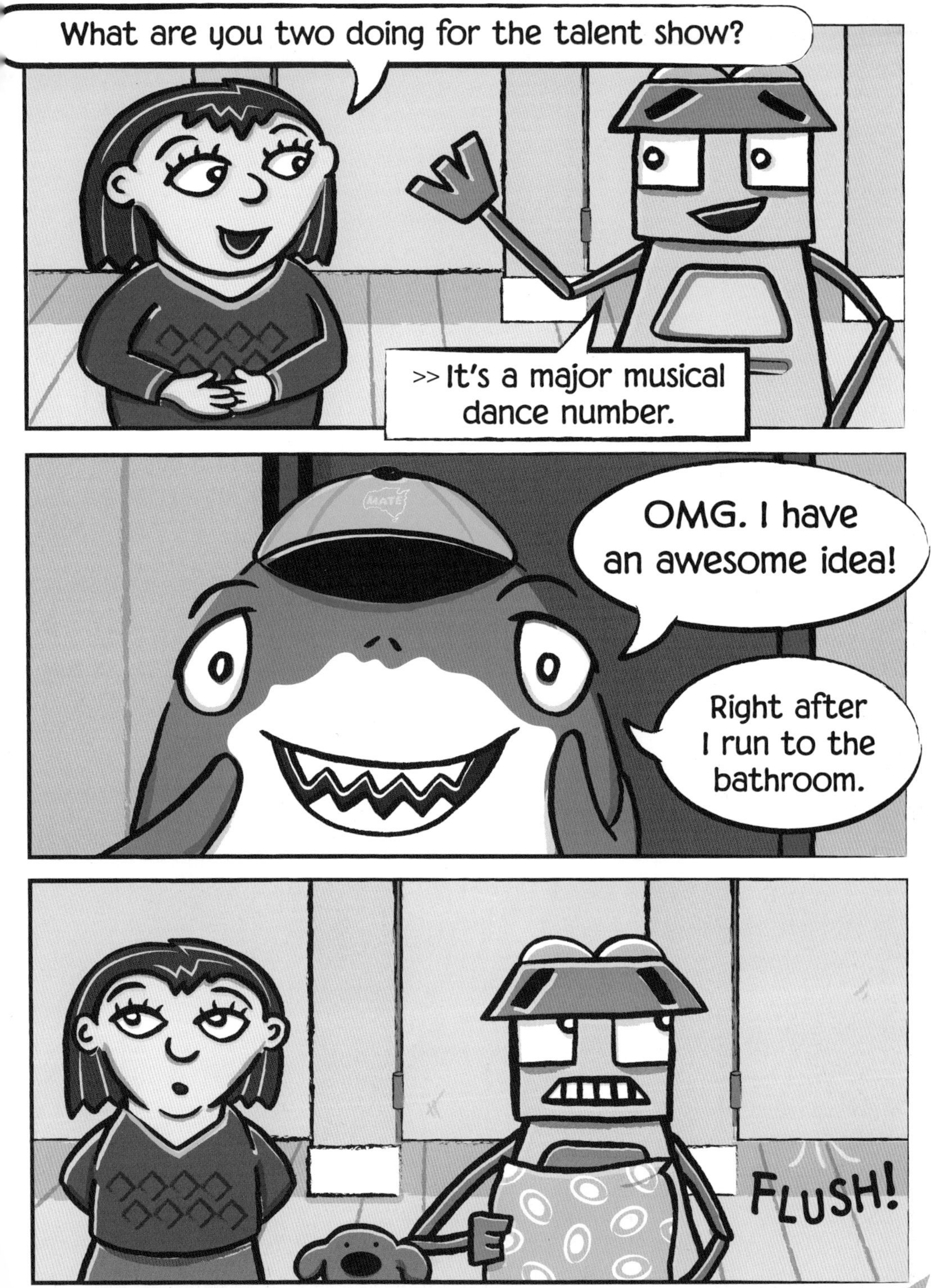
What are you two doing for the talent show?
>> It's a major musical dance number.
OMG. I have an awesome idea!
Right after I run to the bathroom.
FLUSH!

Chapter 8

Summer Camp-ions!

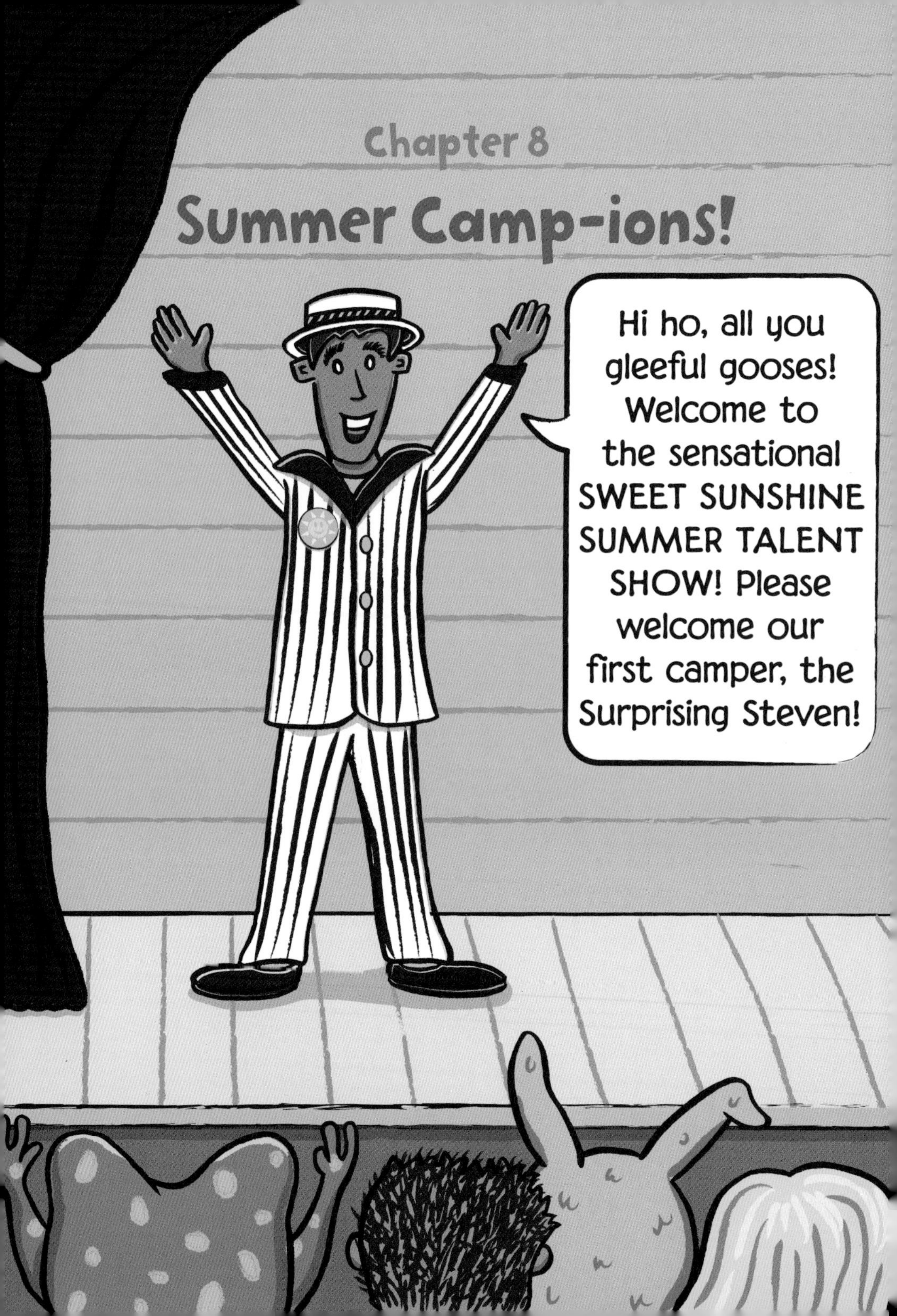

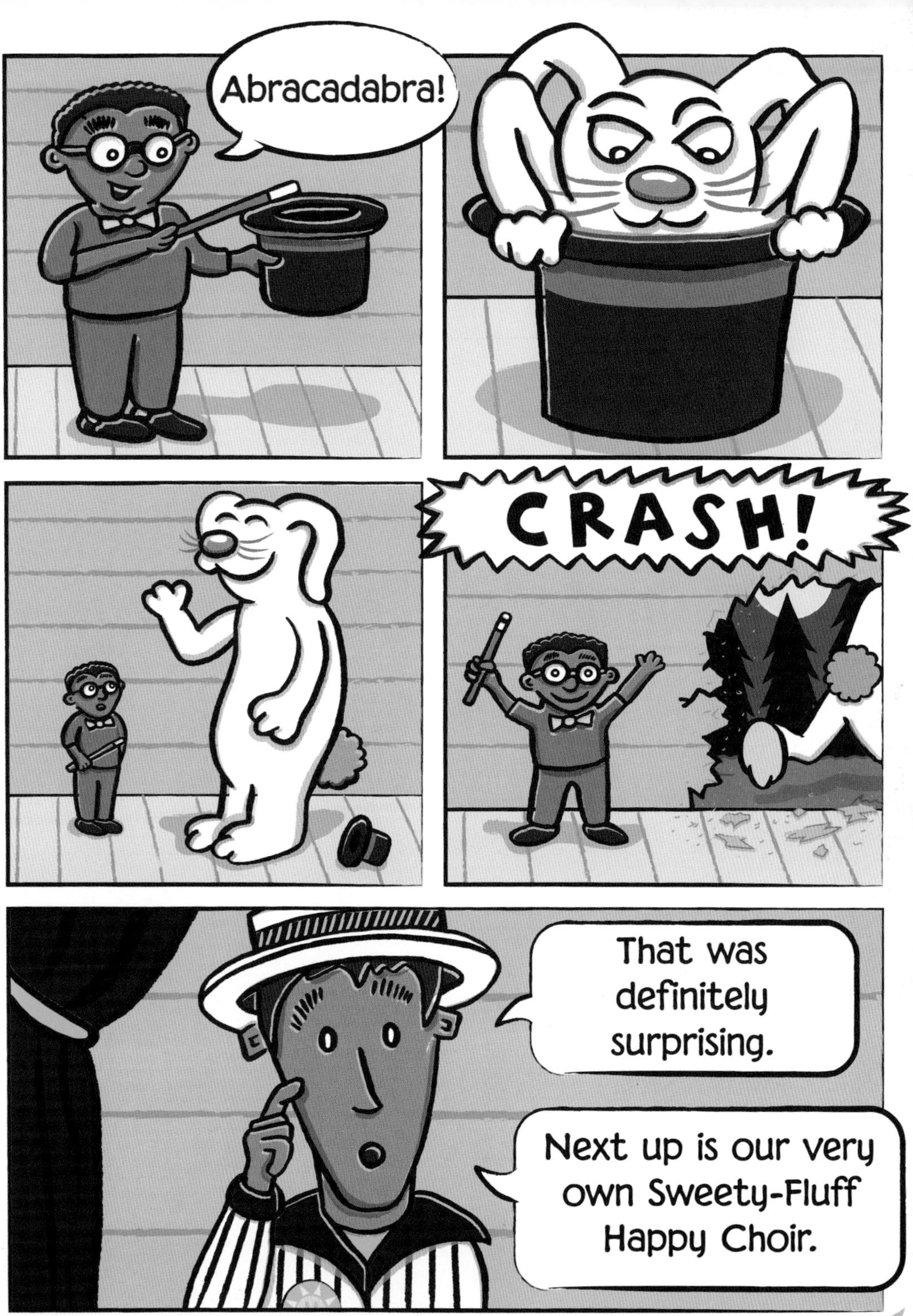
Abracadabra!
CRASH!
That was definitely surprising.
Next up is our very own Sweety-Fluff Happy Choir.

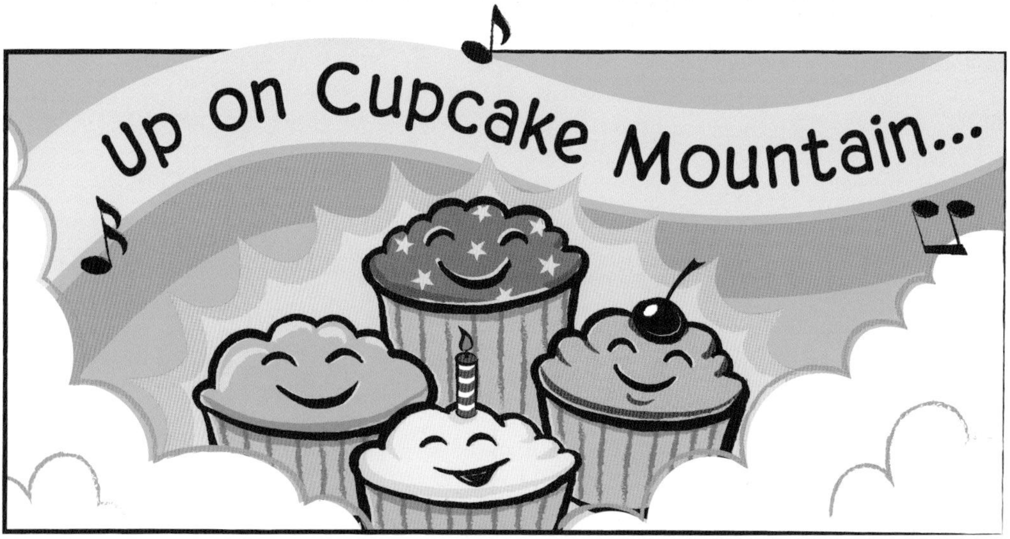
Up on Cupcake Mountain...

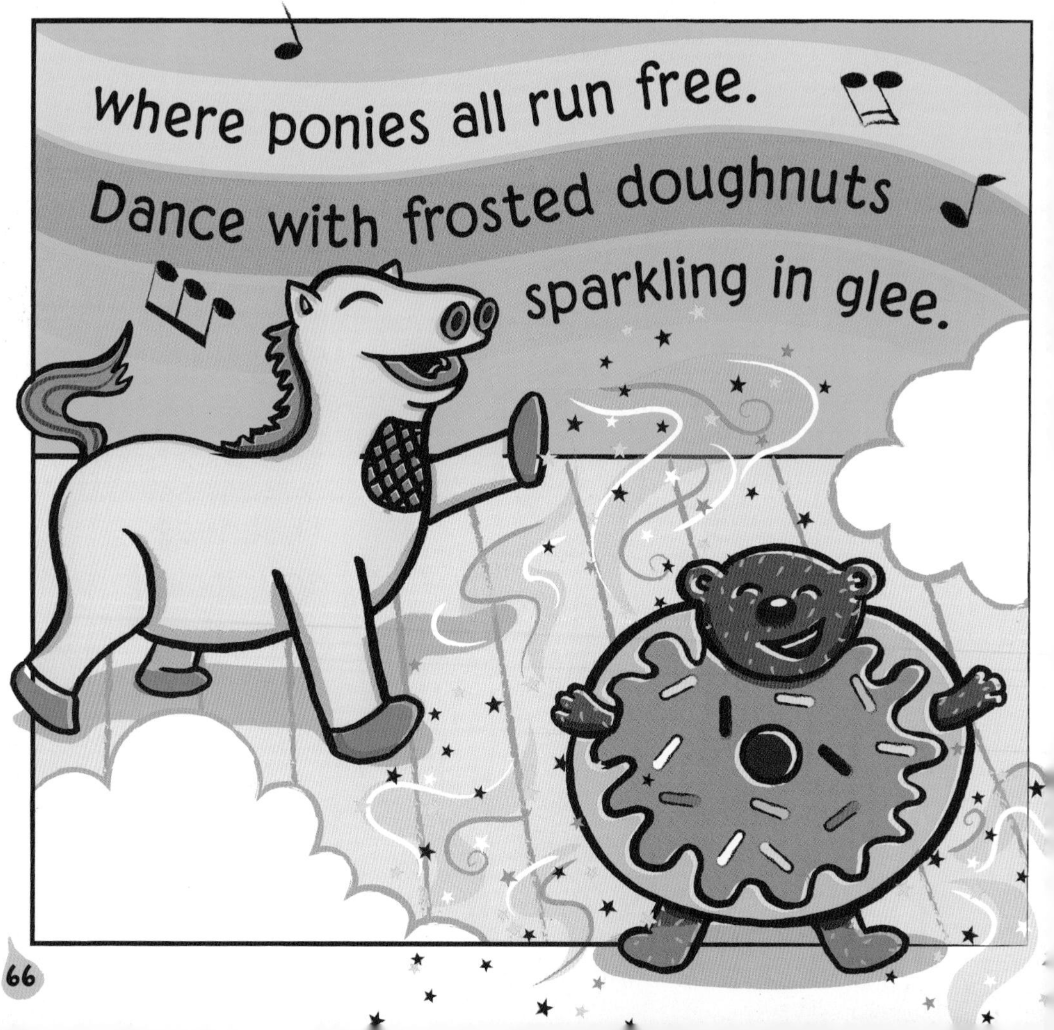
Where ponies all run free.
Dance with frosted doughnuts
sparkling in glee.

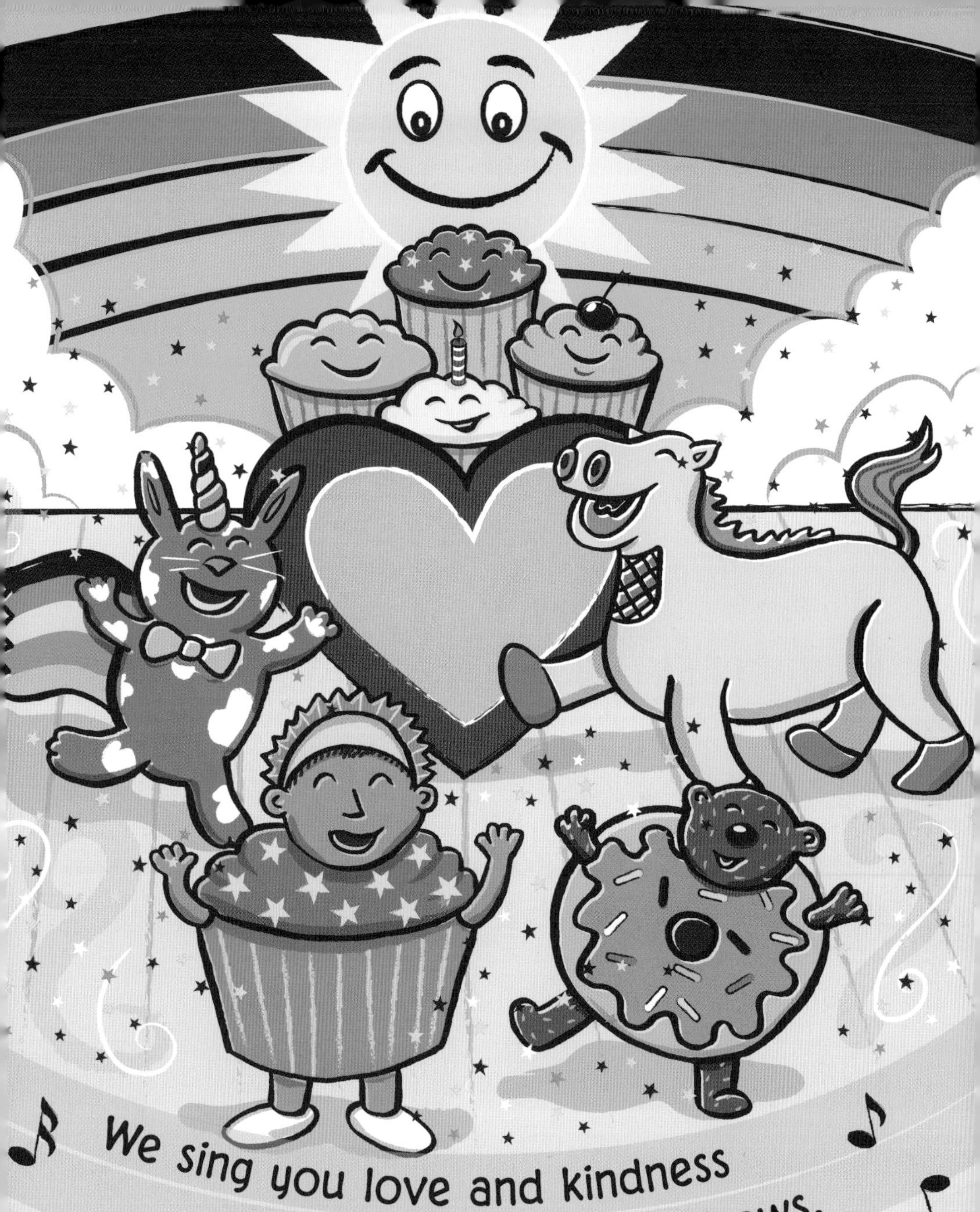

We sing you love and kindness
and bunny-corns with bows.
Our Sweety Sunshine family
together we will grow!

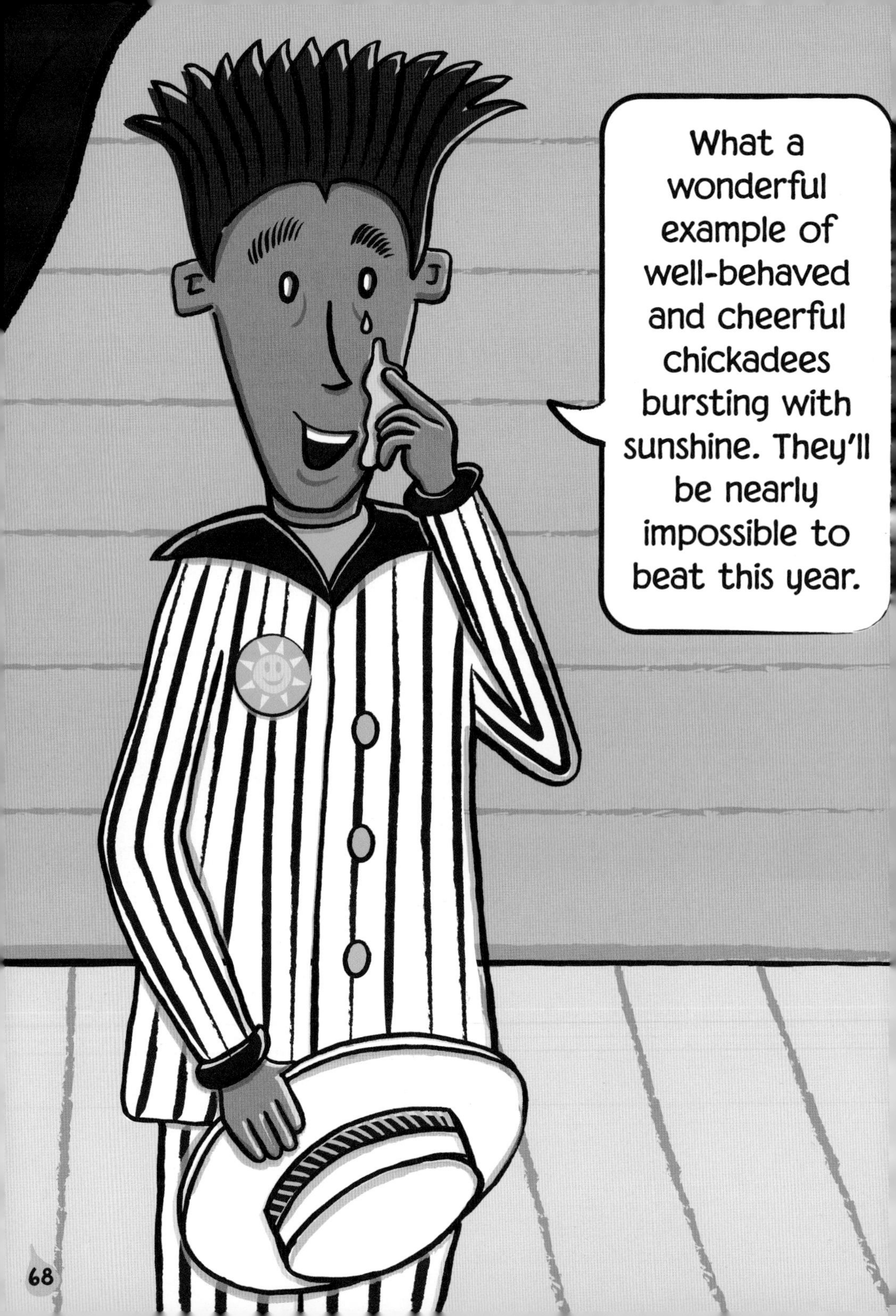
What a wonderful example of well-behaved and cheerful chickadees bursting with sunshine. They'll be nearly impossible to beat this year.

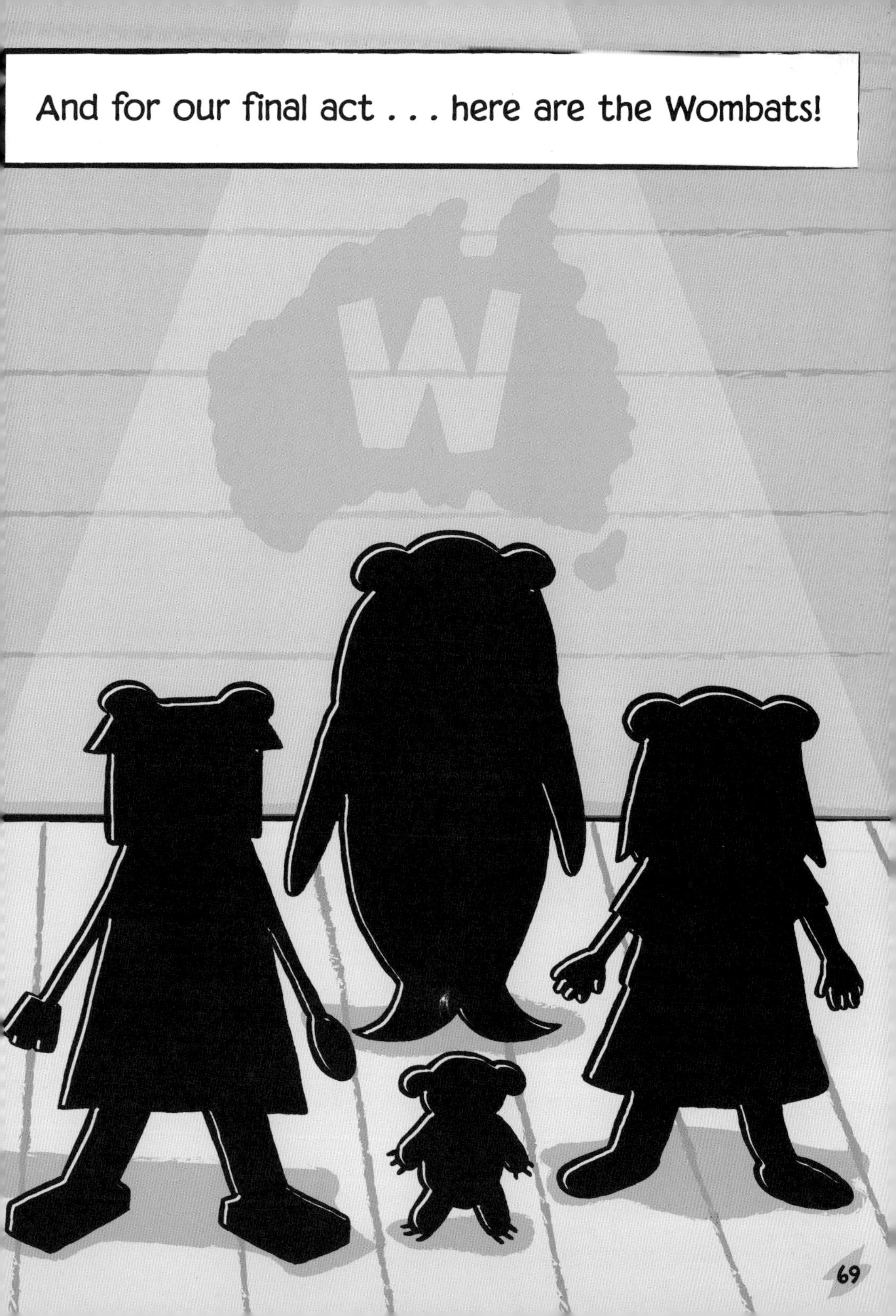
And for our final act . . . here are the Wombats!

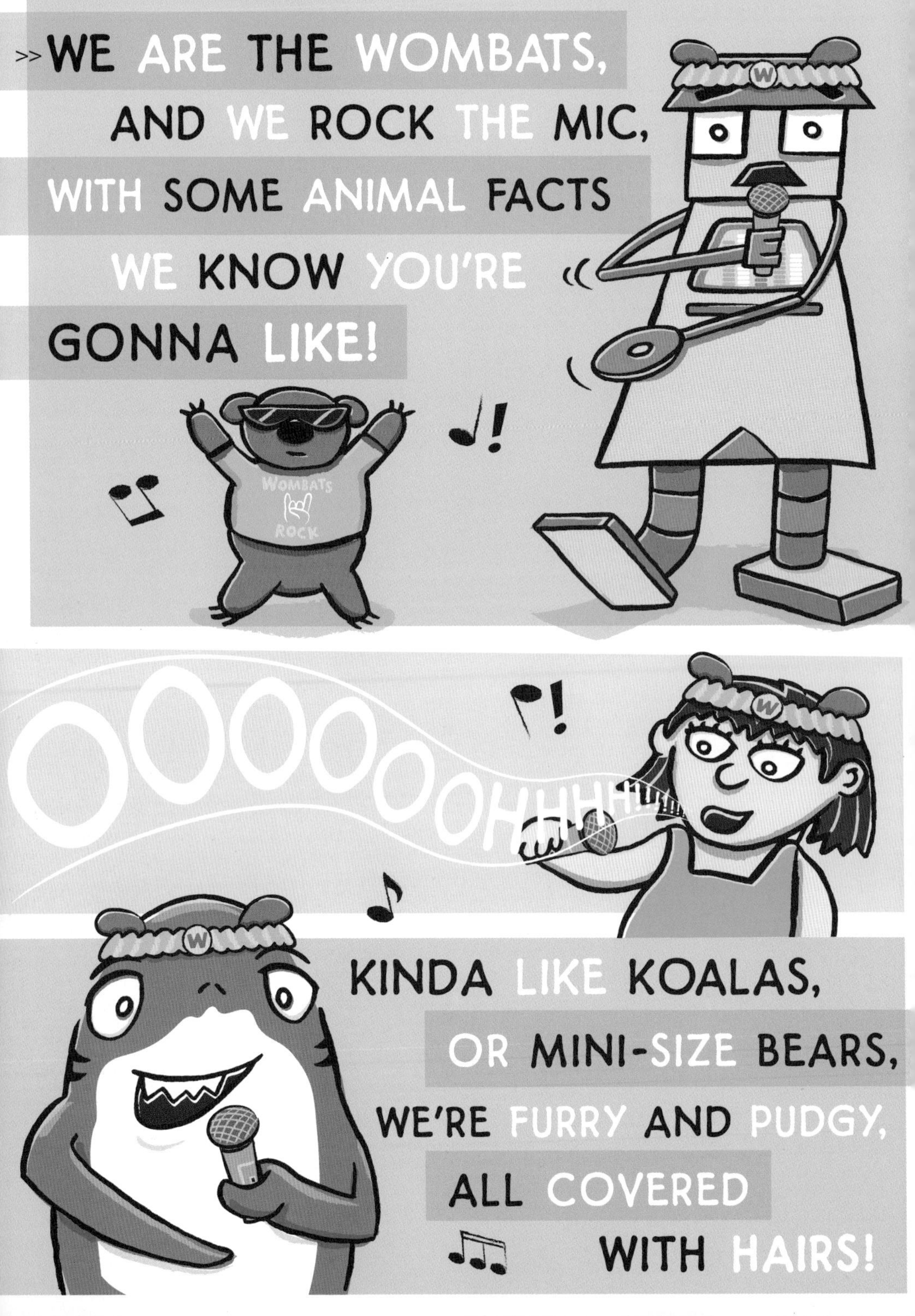
>>WE ARE THE WOMBATS,
AND WE ROCK THE MIC,
WITH SOME ANIMAL FACTS
WE KNOW YOU'RE
GONNA LIKE!
WOMBATS ROCK
OOOOOOOHHHH!!!
KINDA LIKE KOALAS,
OR MINI-SIZE BEARS,
WE'RE FURRY AND PUDGY,
ALL COVERED
WITH HAIRS!

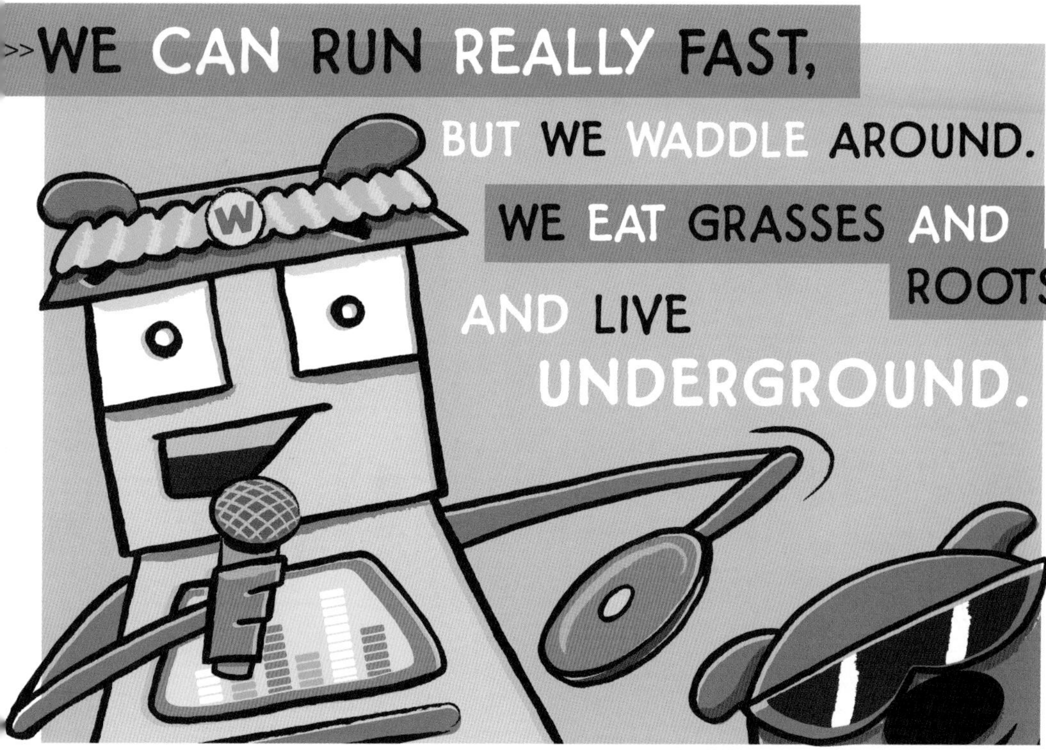
>>WE CAN RUN REALLY FAST,
BUT WE WADDLE AROUND.
WE EAT GRASSES AND ROOTS
AND LIVE UNDERGROUND.

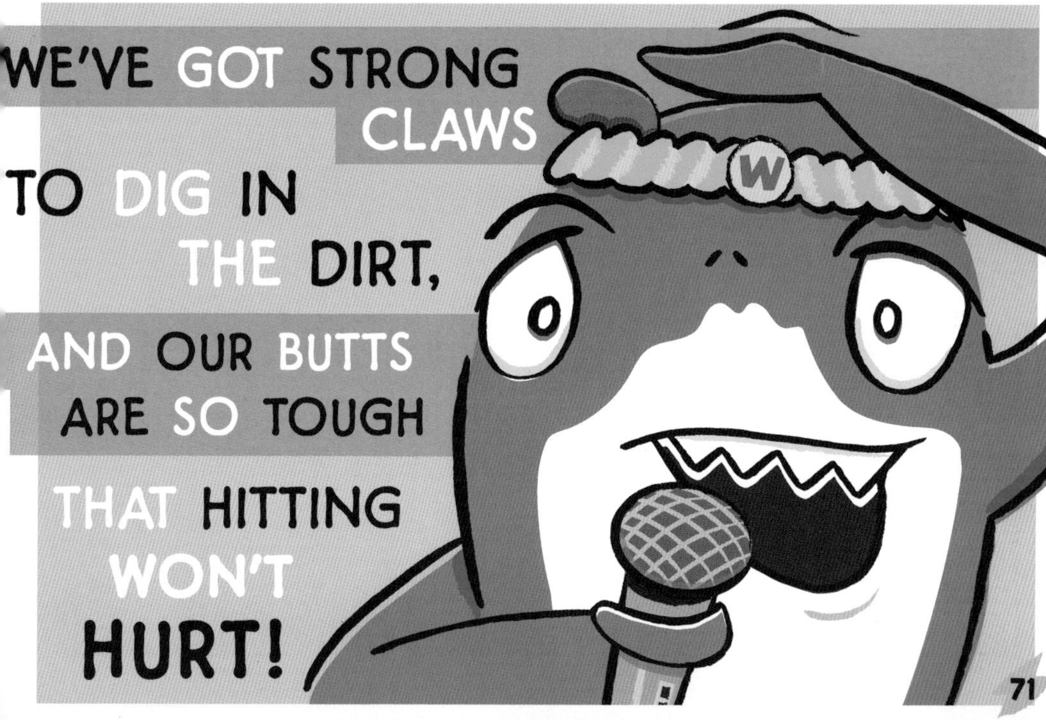
WE'VE GOT STRONG CLAWS
TO DIG IN THE DIRT,
AND OUR BUTTS ARE SO TOUGH
THAT HITTING WON'T HURT!

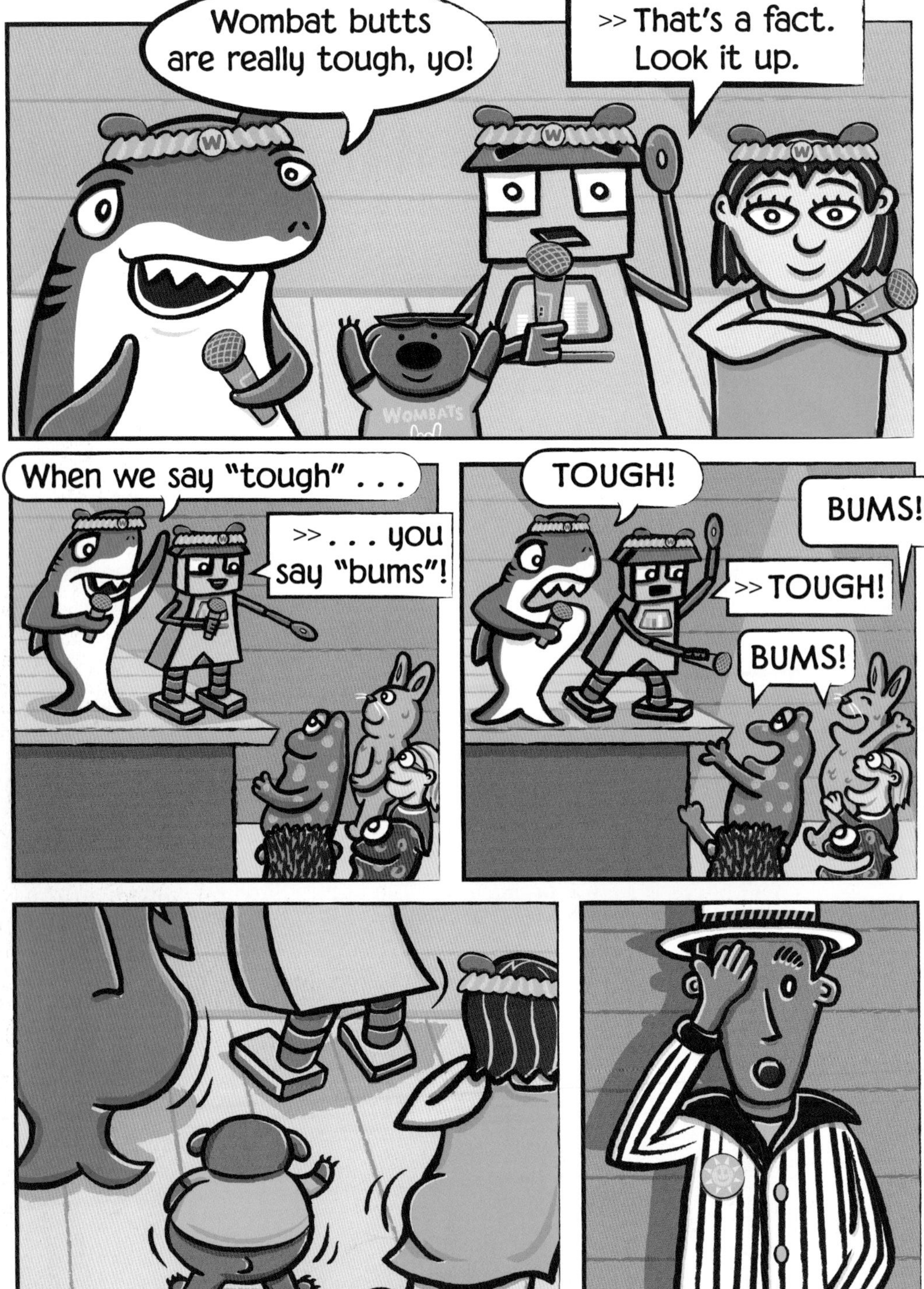

Wombat butts are really tough, yo!
>> That's a fact. Look it up.
WOMBATS
When we say "tough" . . .
>> . . . you say "bums"!
TOUGH!
BUMS!
>> TOUGH!
BUMS!

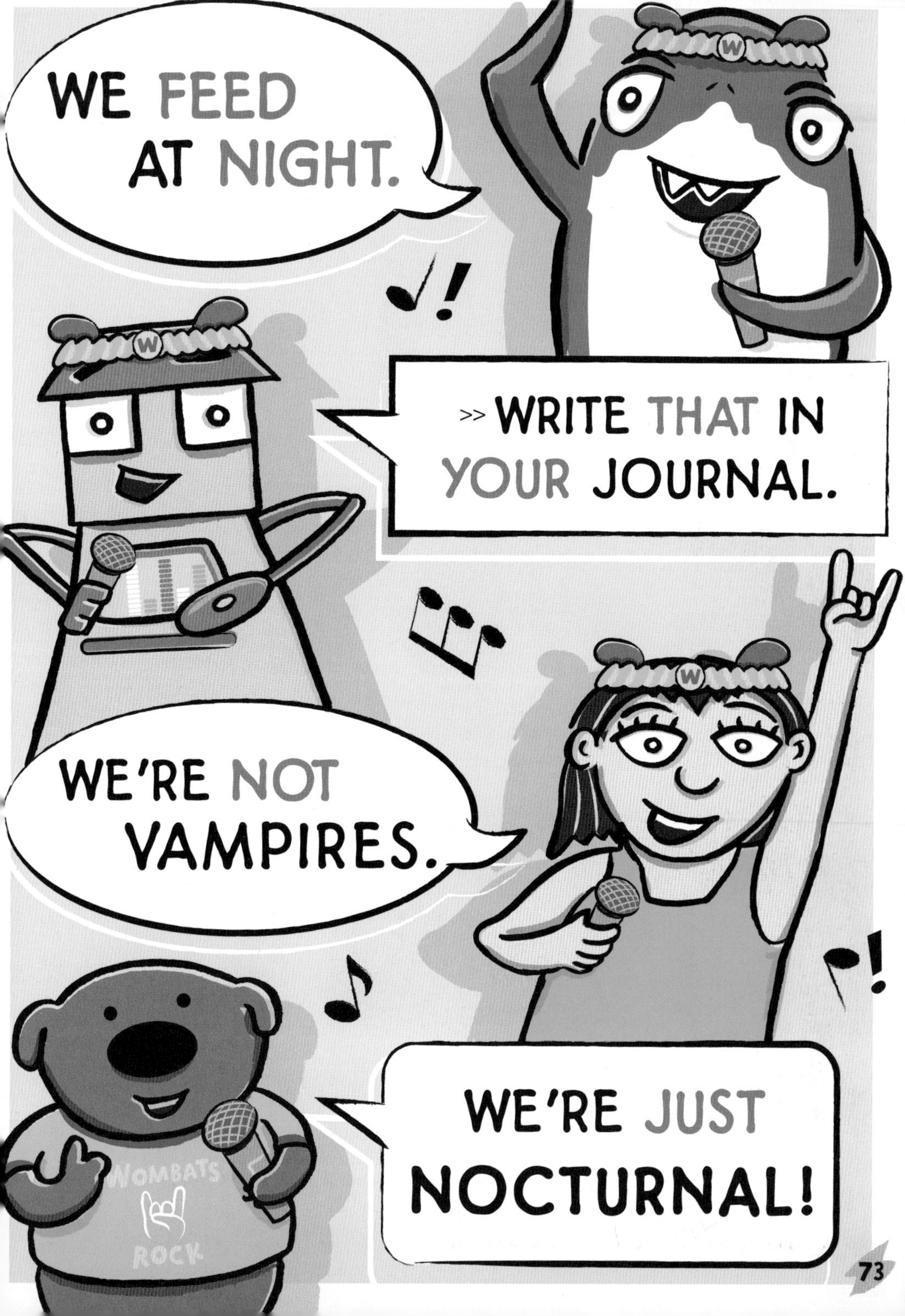
WE FEED AT NIGHT.
>> WRITE THAT IN YOUR JOURNAL.
WE'RE NOT VAMPIRES.
WE'RE JUST NOCTURNAL!
WOMBATS ROCK

WE ARE THE WOMBATS,

AND WE'RE HERE TO SAY...

IT'S TIME TO GO WILD,

SO SHOUT HOORAY!

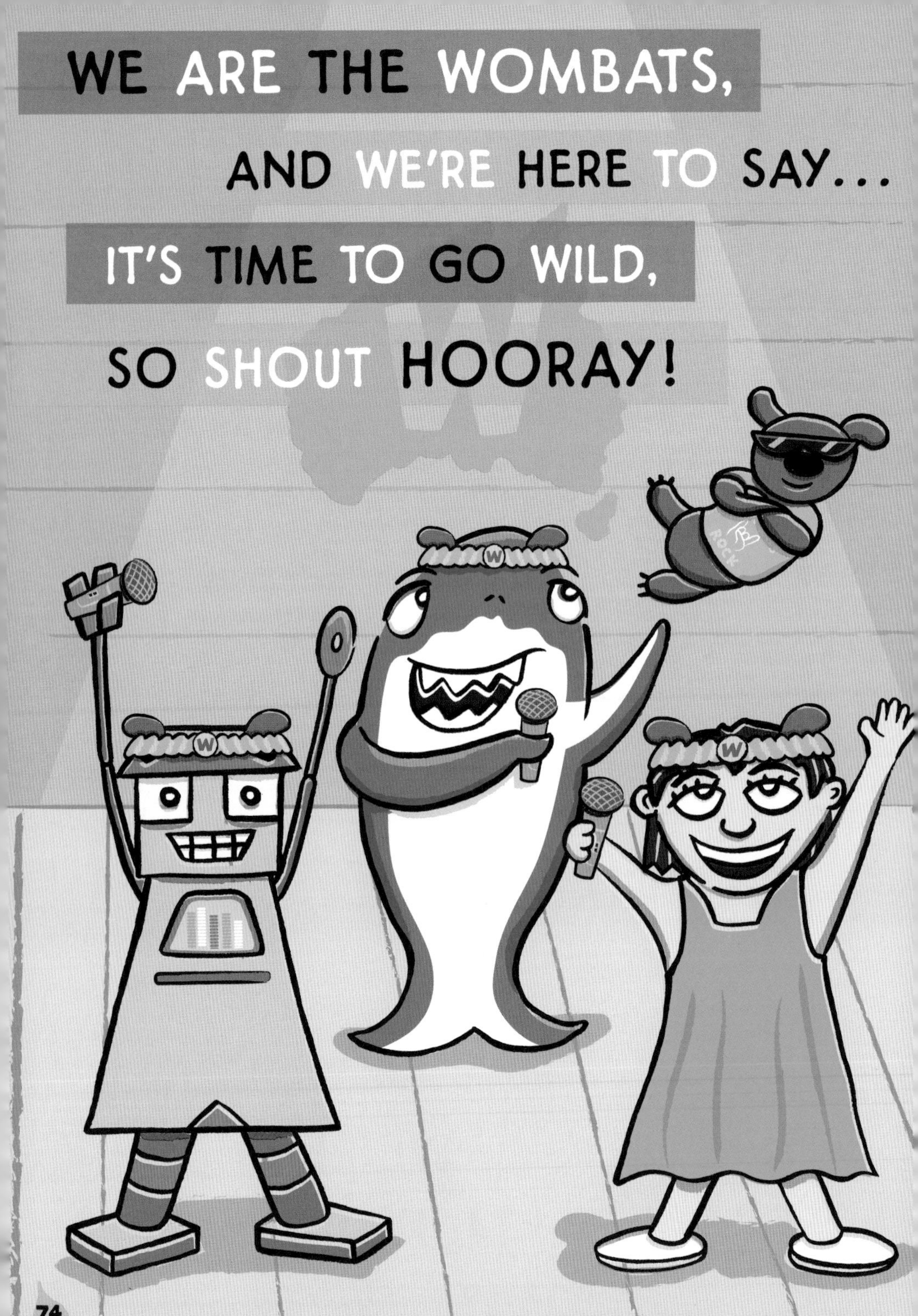
ROCK

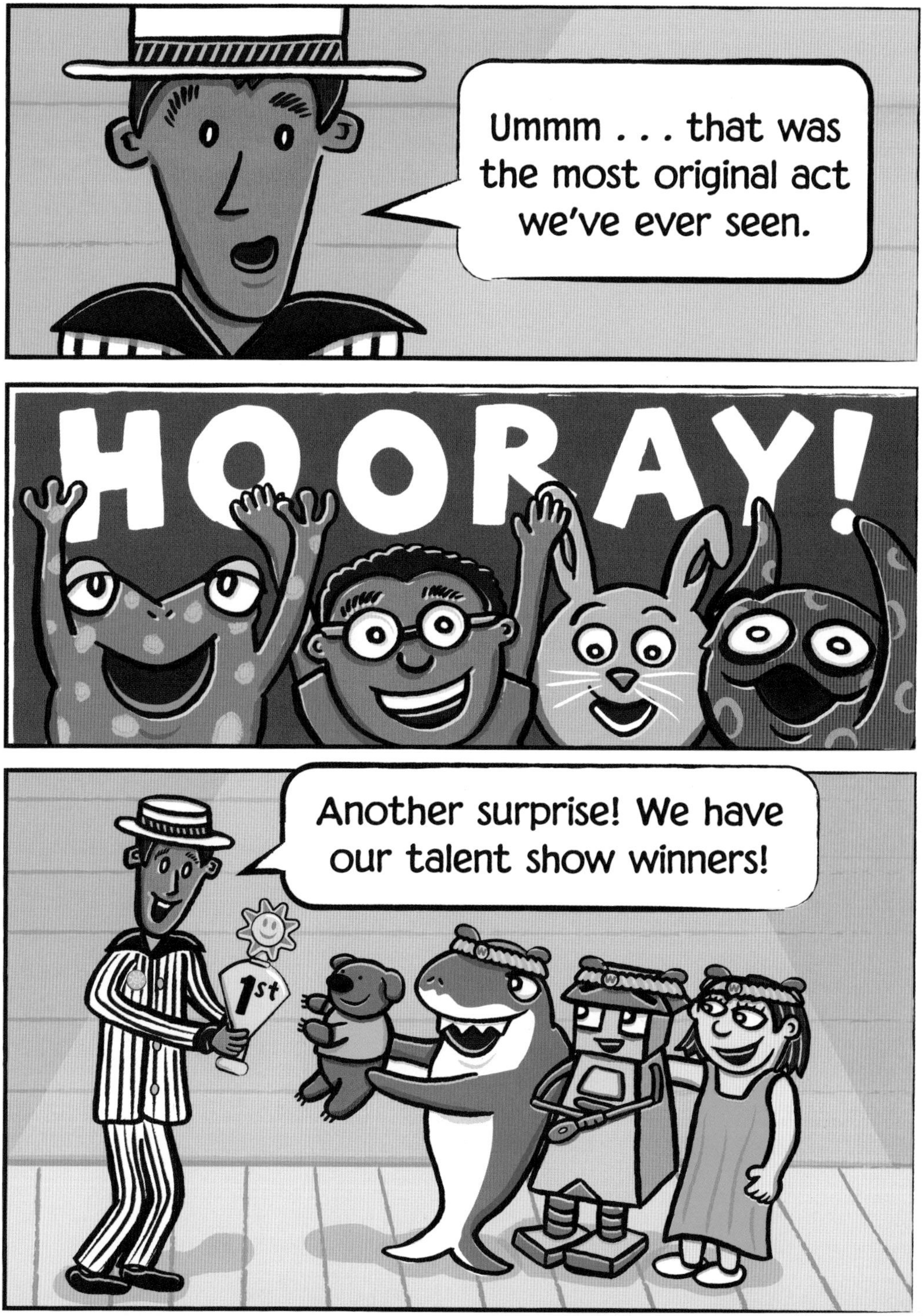
Ummm . . . that was the most original act we've ever seen.
HOORAY!
Another surprise! We have our talent show winners!
1st

SUNSHINE OATH

1. Try new things.

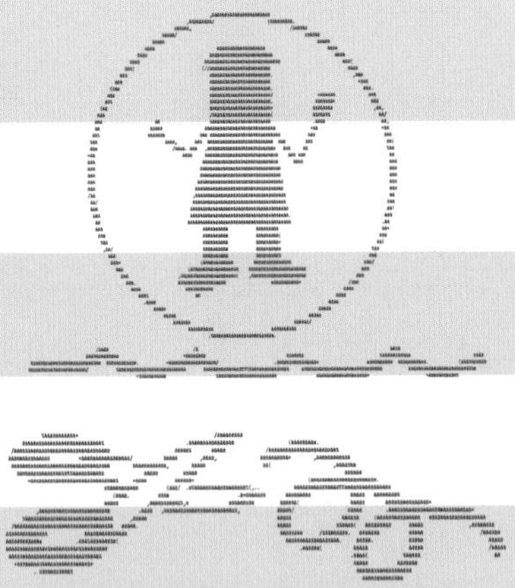

COMPLETE ☑

2. Make new friends.

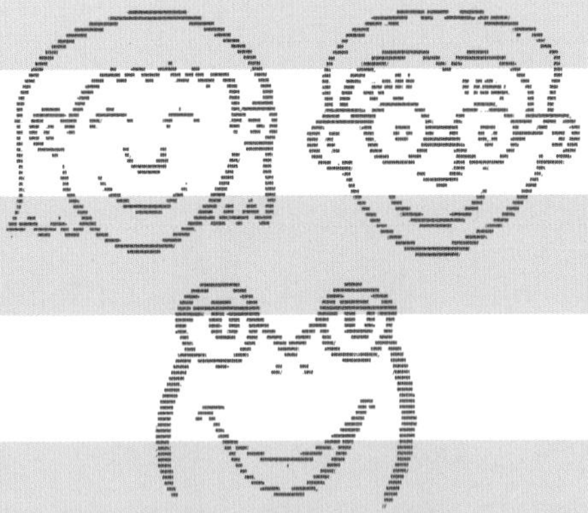

COMPLETE ☑

3. Do a good deed.

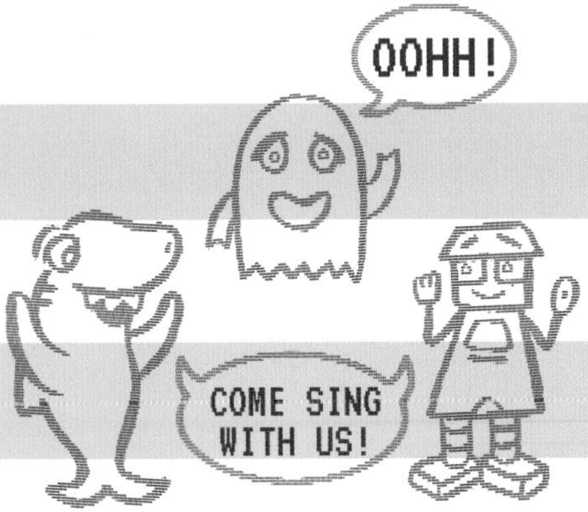
OOHH!
COME SING WITH US!

COMPLETE ☑

4. Make something beautiful.

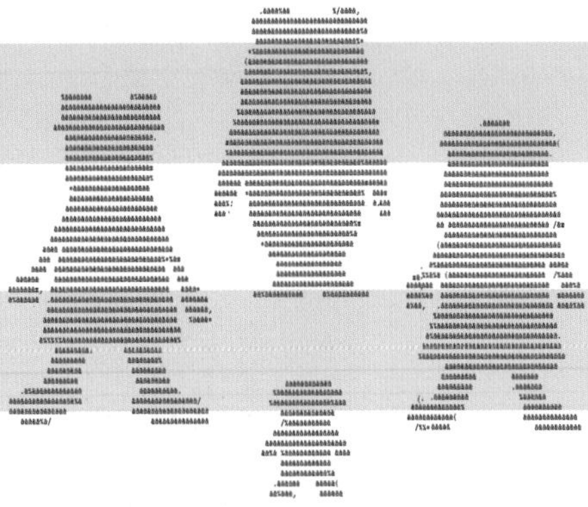

COMPLETE ☑

5. Give free hugs.

COMPLETE ☐

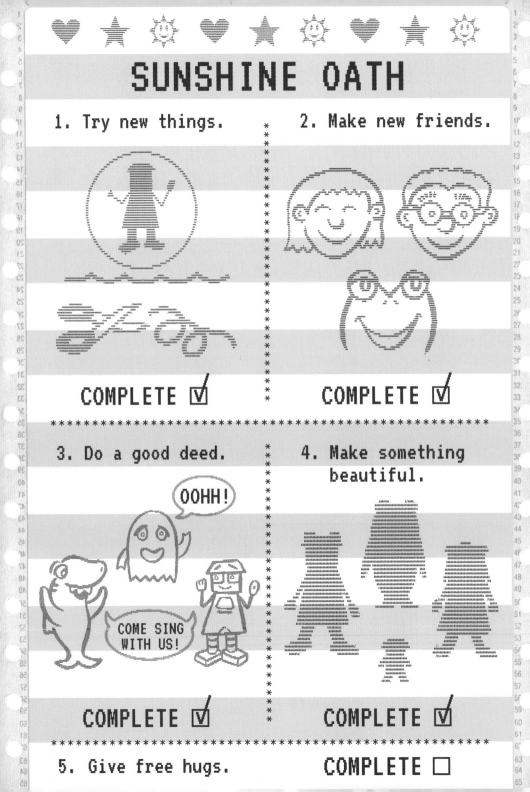

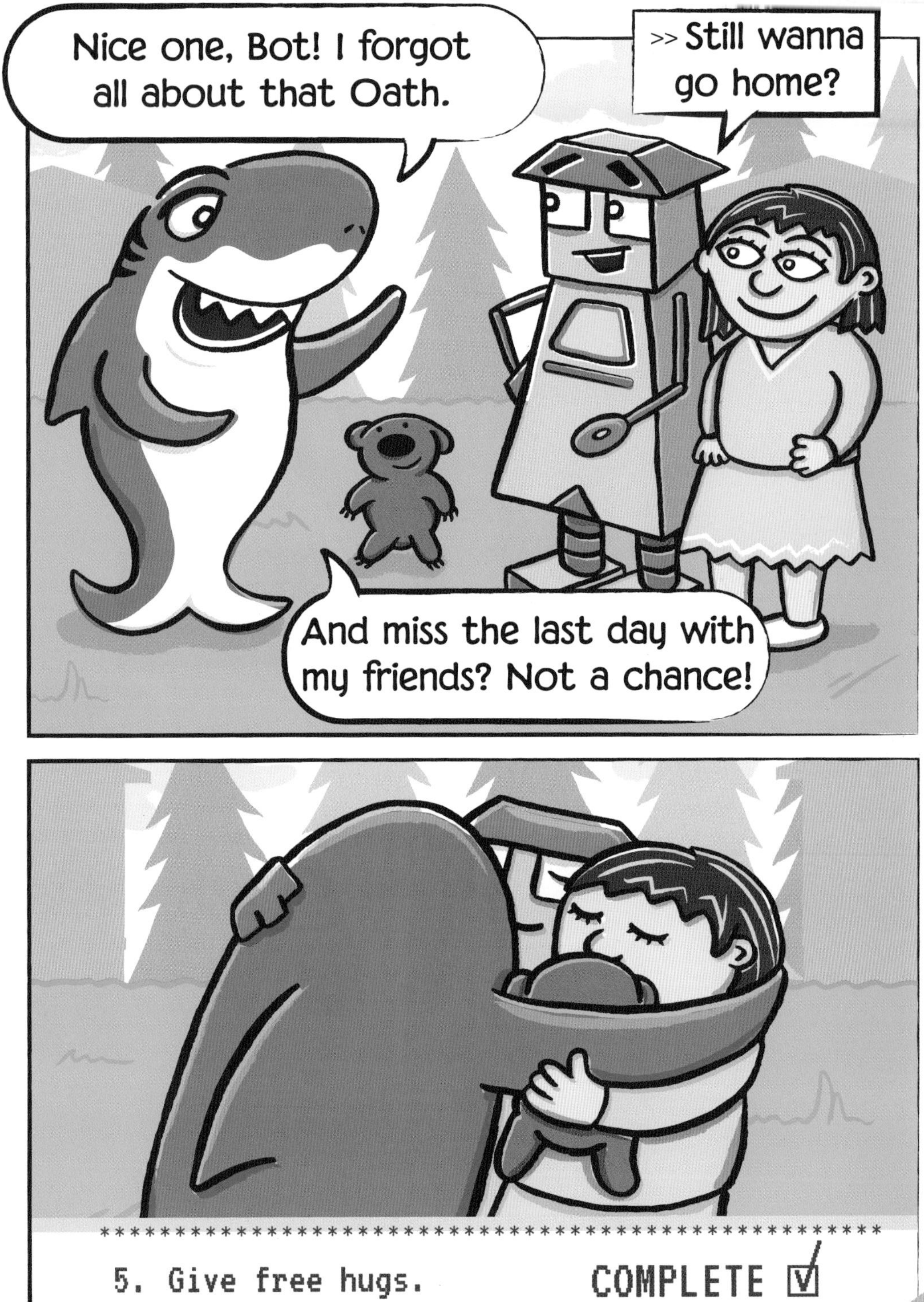
Nice one, Bot! I forgot all about that Oath.
>> Still wanna go home?
And miss the last day with my friends? Not a chance!
****
5. Give free hugs.
COMPLETE ☑

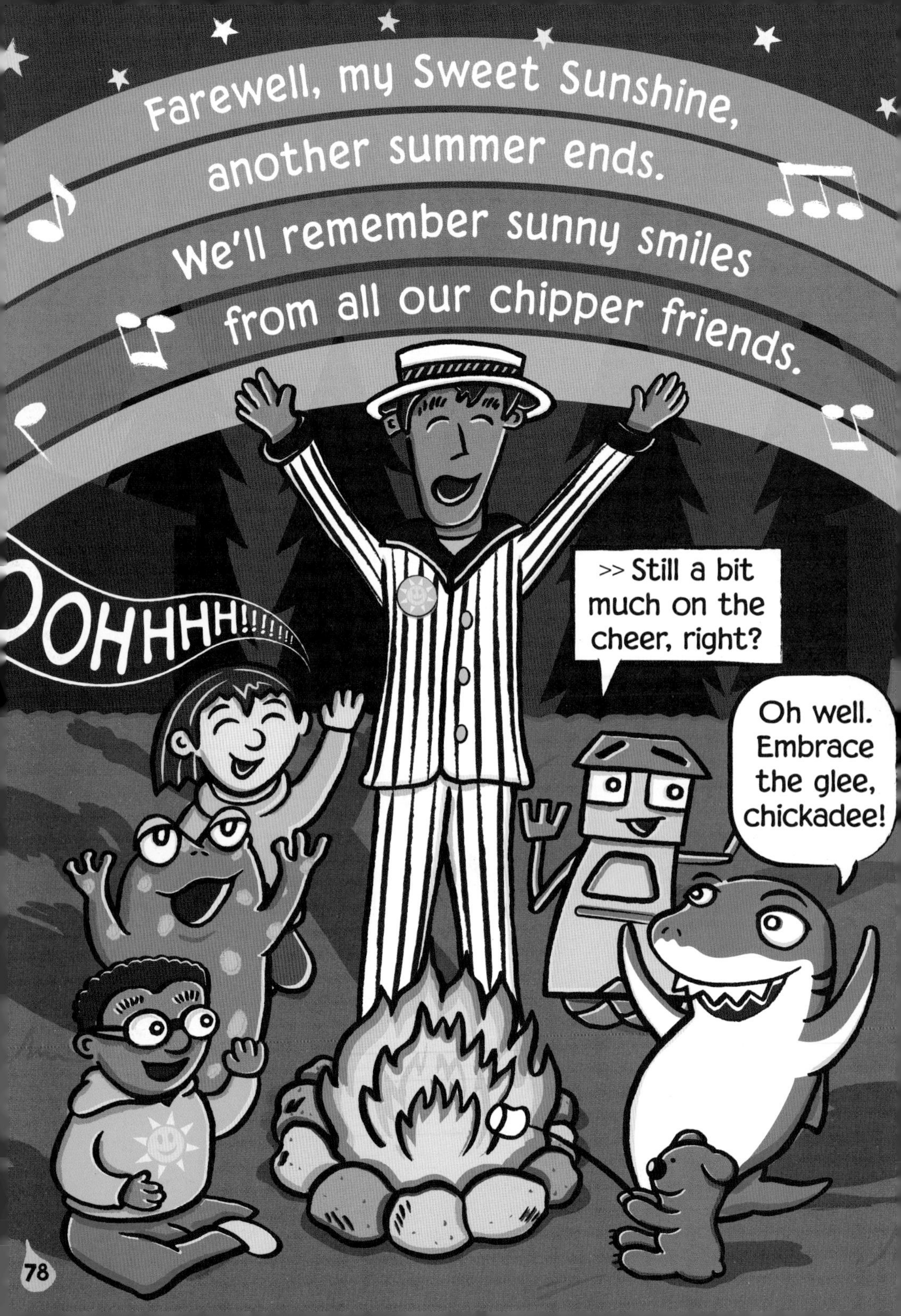
Farewell, my Sweet Sunshine,
another summer ends.
We'll remember sunny smiles
from all our chipper friends.
OOHHHH!!!!!!
>> Still a bit much on the cheer, right?
Oh well. Embrace the glee, chickadee!

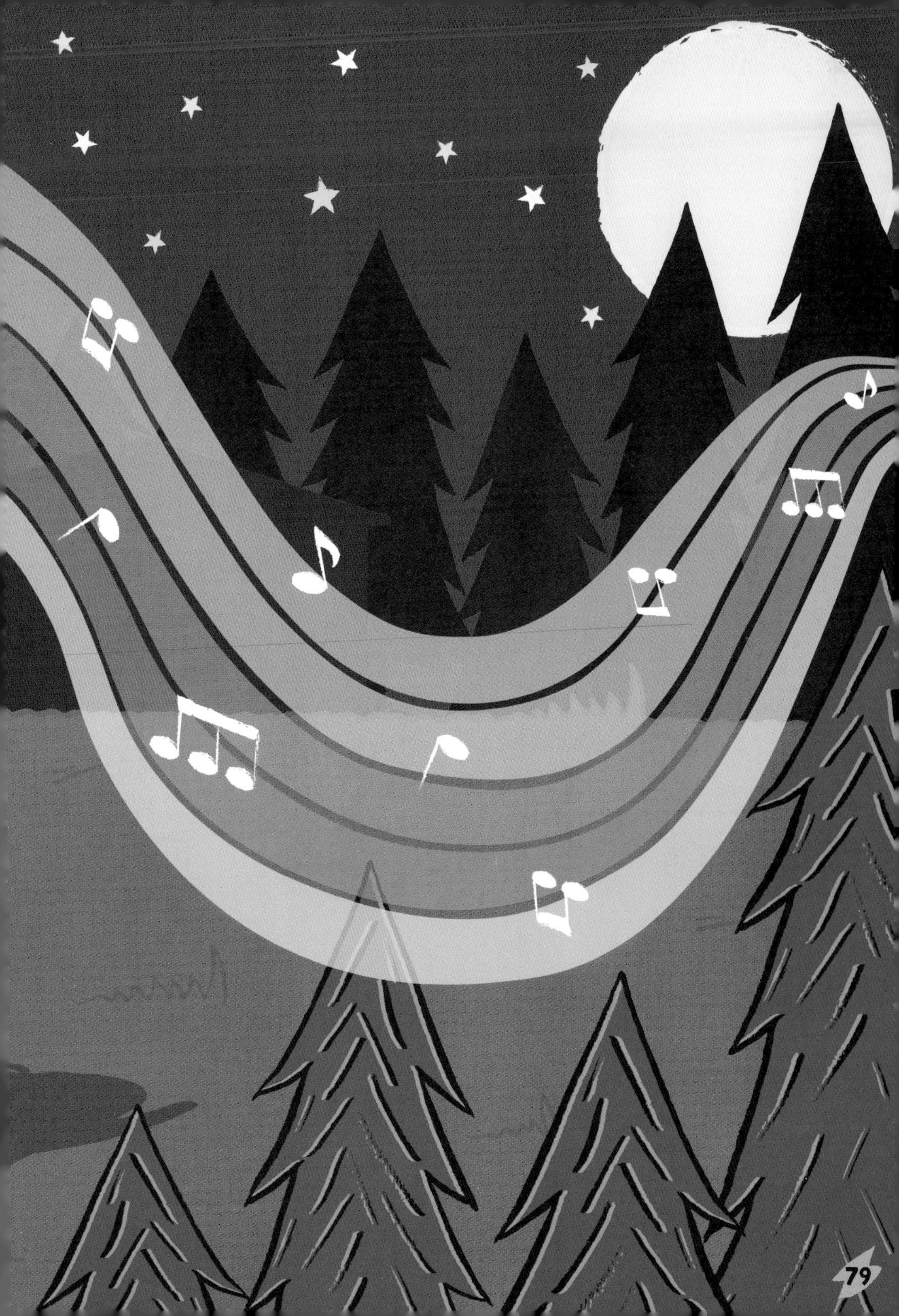

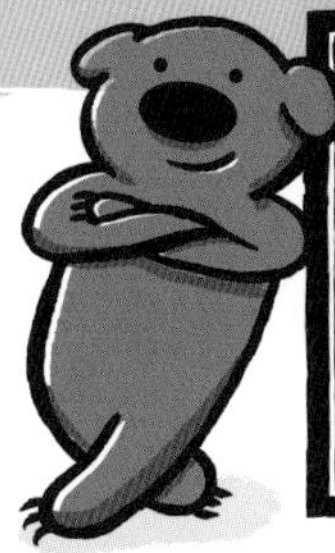

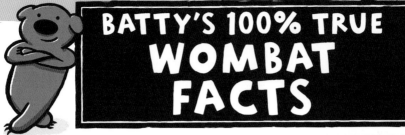

BATTY'S 100% TRUE WOMBAT FACTS

Vombatus ursinus (common wombat)

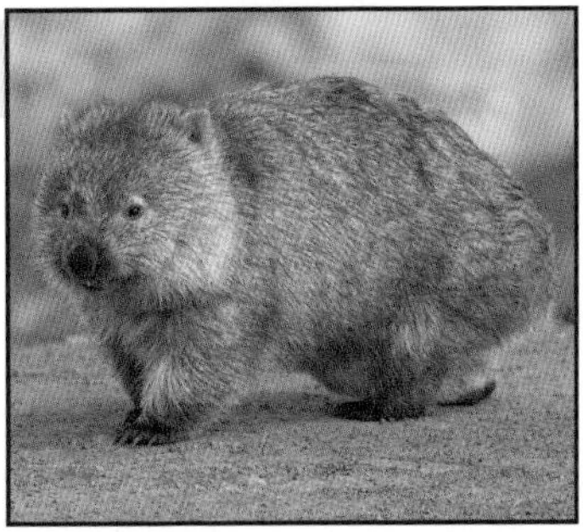

- Native to Australia
- Short, pudgy, muscular, covered in fur, long claws
- DIET: grasses, herbs, roots, bark
- Mostly NOCTURNAL (come out at night to feed)

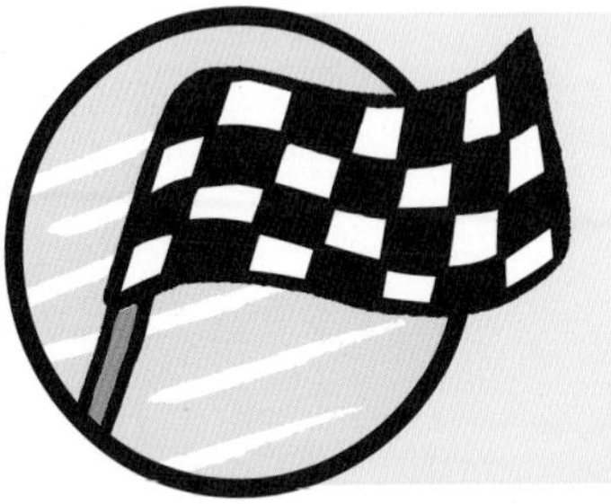

SPEED WADDLER

Although they waddle, a wombat can probably beat you in a race. They can run up to 25 miles per hour.

FAST FANGS

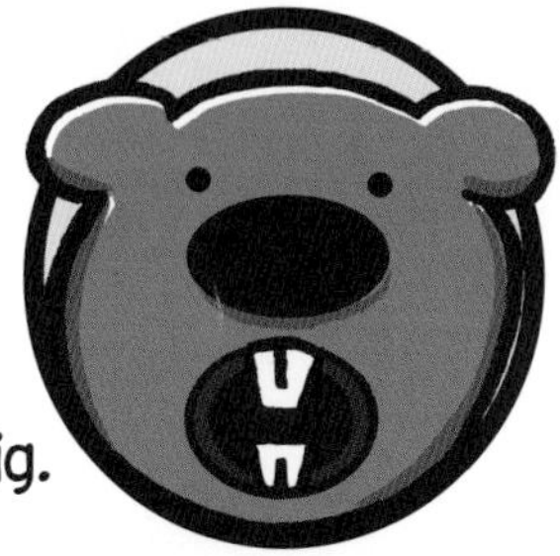

A wombat's front teeth (incisors) never stop growing. Wombats gnaw on hard things like roots to keep their teeth from getting too big.

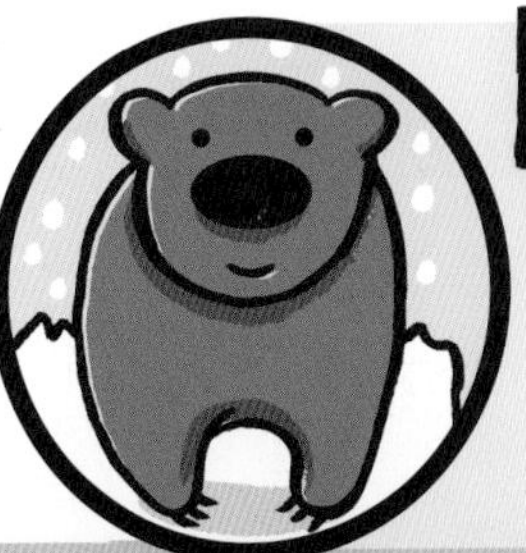

GRANDMA WAS HUGE

Around 2.4 million years ago, during the Ice Age, "giant wombats" the size of a rhinoceros roamed Australia.

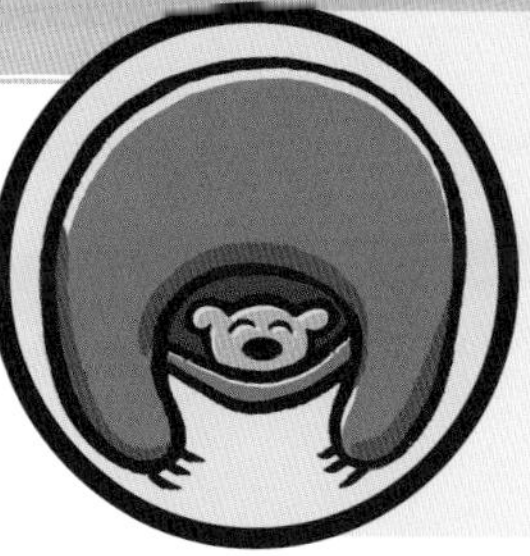

BABY BACK POCKET

A wombat has a pouch (called a marsupium) on its backside where its baby grows after being born. (Kangaroos have their pouch on the front.)

SUPER DIGGER

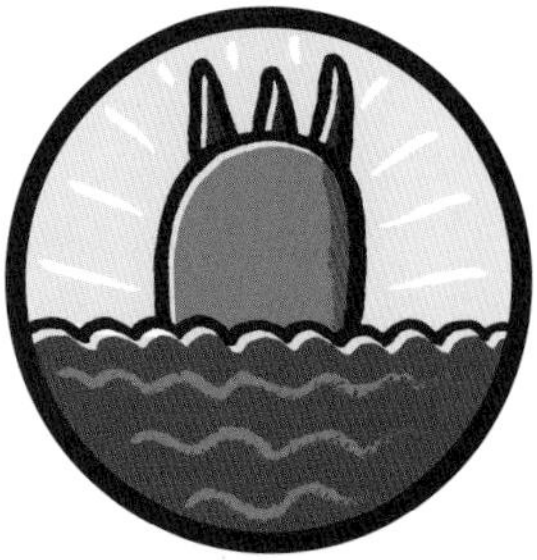

With strong feet, long claws, and short muscular bodies, wombats are awesome at digging tunnels and burrows.

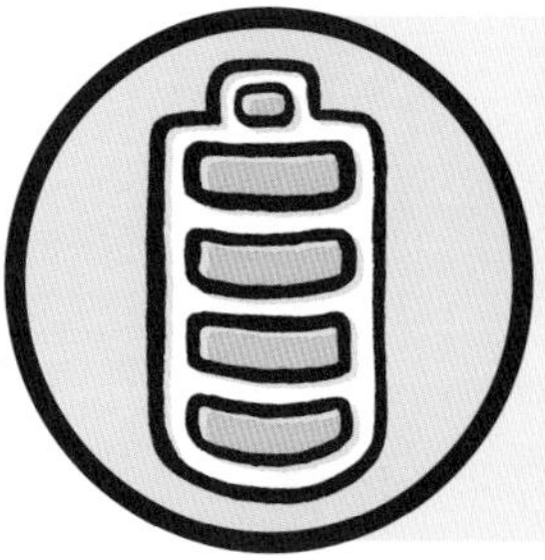

ENERGY SAVER

It can take up to 14 days for a wombat to digest a meal. (It takes humans about six to eight hours.) This helps a wombat conserve energy in a hot environment.

BUM SHIELD

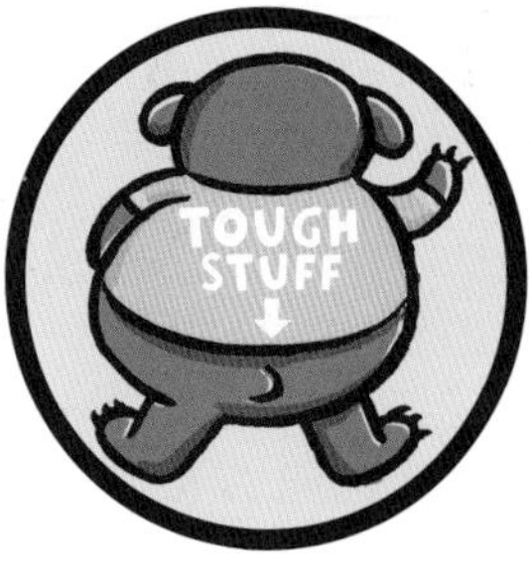
TOUGH
STUFF

The rumps of wombats are made of cartilage (very tough tissue) and can be used for protection by blocking the entrance to a tunnel.

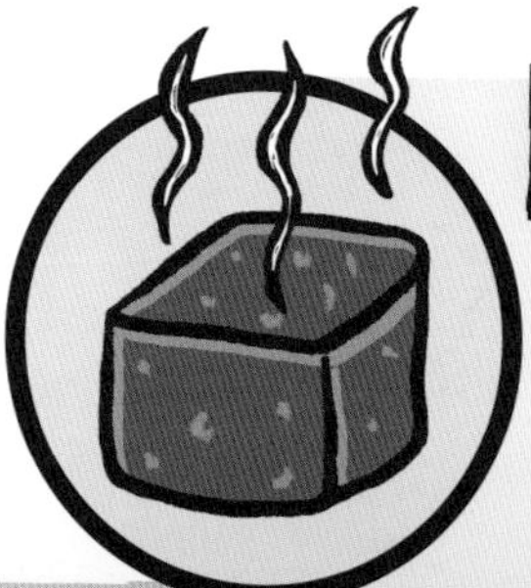

CUBE POOPER

Wombats have special bones in their backsides that create square-shaped poop.

HOW TO DRAW BATTY

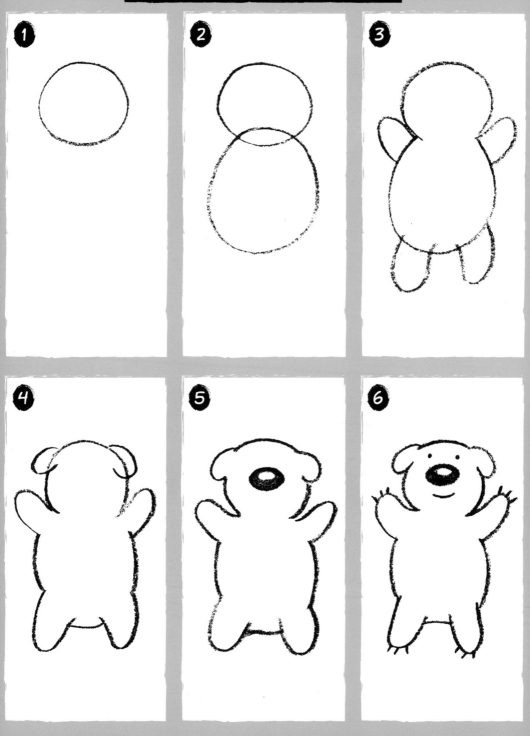

Brian Yanish has worked for Jim Henson Productions, trained as a special effects mold maker, written and performed comedy, and designed educational software, apparel, furniture, and toys. He is the creator of ScrapKins®, a recycled arts program that inspires kids to see creative potential in everyday junk. Brian has presented workshops at schools around the world and even appeared on *Sesame Street.* He lives in Rochester, New York, and enjoys sharks, robots, and gummy things.

brianyanish.com